Illustrated **Timmi TOBBSON** Adventure

# SECRETS OF THE LAST PIRATE

by J. I. WAGNER          Illustrated by J. G. RATTI

*For those who keep a twinkle in their eyes,*

*love in their hearts*

*and daydreams in their minds.*

Written by J. I. Wagner.

Illustrated by J. G. Ratti.

Translated into English by Elani Koogle Wales. Edited by Grace Glowiak.

Book design © by Freude am Buch GmbH based on a layout from BookDesignTemplates.com.


Published by Evergreen Books.

(formerly named freshabooks)

Printed in Canada.

Evergreen Books is an imprint of:

Freude am Buch GmbH
Robert-Bosch-Str. 32
63303 Dreieich, Germany

www.timmitobbson.com

www.evergreen-books.de

Publisher's Note: This is a work of fiction. Names, characters, places, and incidents are a product of the author's imagination. Locales and public names are sometimes used for atmospheric purposes. Any resemblance to actual people, living or dead, or to businesses, companies, events, institutions, or locales is completely coincidental.

Hardcover: TBD
Paperback: ISBN 978-3-96326-755-0
E-Book: 978-3-96326-750-5

Printed in 2022.

# Get the Fan-Package for FREE!

Go to TimmiTobbson.com to get your free downloads of the **"Easter-Egg-Companion"**, **"The Art of Secrets"** as well as the **"Numbers Cheatbook"**. (Available as PDF-files.)

## https://timmitobbson.com/fan-package-secrets/

# Welcome to the World of Timmi Tobbson!

This is your adventure, first and foremost. Choose wisely to master each challenge. The magnifying glasses indicate what Timmi, Lilli and Marvin think about the difficulty of each puzzle.

Normal:     Hard:     Ultimate:

This is just their opinion. Maybe you will find a puzzle easy that they find hard or the other way around.

❖ ❖ ❖

You will find hints in the back of this book that can help you solve the upcoming picture mysteries.

❖ ❖ ❖

The solution to each puzzle is revealed in the subsequent chapter.

❖ ❖ ❖

You might find the following tools helpful, though they are not required to solve the puzzles:

Magnifying glass  ❖  Pen  ❖  Small mirror to read the hints section (mirror writing)  ❖  **Flashlight (for reading in the dark)**

# The Chapters

The Night Before ............................................ 4

The Sunken Treasure Ship ................................7

Genius à la Lotterlulu.....................................12

The Dive ......................................................16

A Restless Night ..........................................20

Now Or Never ..............................................24

The Treasure Chamber....................................28

Star Island .................................................32

Hot On the Heels ..........................................36

Outsmarted .................................................40

The Prisoner ...............................................46

Under Observation ........................................50

The Bank of Pirates.......................................54

The Calm Before the Storm..............................58

Attack of the Guardians .................................64

The Escape..................................................68

Deep Inside the Cliffs ....................................72

A Casket Full of Puzzles.................................78

Protect and Serve .........................................82

The Code.....................................................86

Descent Into Darkness....................................90

The Needle in the Haystack.............................94

Among the Guardians .....................................98

The Plan....................................................102

In the Trap.................................................106

The Lion's Den.............................................110

The Last Pirate...........................................114

Code Red....................................................120

A Narrow Escape..........................................124

Not Quite Fair ...........................................128

The Last Battle ..........................................134

Settling the Score........................................142

A New Beginning ..........................................150

A Cup of Cocoa ...........................................156

Timmi

Hi, I'm Timmi.

I may not be the most confident kid. Or the most athletic. But I am curious. And that's definitely worth something.

Lilli

This is Lilli.

Lilli is one of my two best friends. She can be really stubborn. And cheeky. But most of all, she's the bravest person I know. She would do anything to help a friend in need.

Marvin

This is Marvin.

He is my other best friend. He loves animals. When he's happy, he jumps up and down. And claps. It looks really funny, but he doesn't care.

# What Happened Previously

## Timmi Tobbson No. 1:
## Legend of the Star Runner

With the help of the treasure hunter Sir London, Timmi, Lilli and Marvin discovered the pirate ship *Star Runner*, thought lost for centuries. The galleon was once the pride and joy of the legendary pirate Lotterlulu and on board were clues to a hidden treasure. But instead of gold and jewels, the children ultimately found a very special book called *El Iksir* (translated: Elixir). Before they could uncover the secrets of the book, it was snatched away from them by a mysterious organization, the Guardians of the Dark Power. According to legend, these Guardians could be recognized by their dark eyes and black mouth. Why they have this eerie discoloration is still a mystery, but instead the children revealed another secret: Lilli is a direct descendant of the pirate Lotterlulu.

## After *Legend* and Before *Legacy*

The discovery of the Star Runner was hailed as a minor sensation by scientists around the world. The ship was studied carefully, but it was badly damaged and restoration would have cost a fortune. Eventually, it was bought by an anonymous collector and taken out of the country to an unknown location.

# Timmi Tobbson No. 2:
# Legacy of the Inventor

Lilli learned about a treasure hunt set up by the famous inventor James Eckles, who had recently disappeared without a trace. The clues also revolved around an elixir. Was this a coincidence?

It quickly became clear that this time, too, the Guardians of the Dark Power were involved.

One of their top commanders, a certain Dr. Sangrey, had forced the inventor James Eckles to create an elixir based on the book El Iksir. This elixir could open the human mind, making it possible to acquire enormous knowledge and impressive abilities in a very short amount of time.

The Guardians of the Dark Power wanted to use the elixir for their own purposes, while James Eckles wanted to make it available to the whole world. For that reason, the inventor hid a few samples in a safe place.

In the end, however, Dr. Sangrey managed to destroy the samples. Timmi and his friends did not learn whether the Guardians could now make the elixir on their own, without the help of the rescued inventor. Dr. Sangrey was arrested by Inspector Hallewell, who the three had met during the course of the adventure.

## After *Legacy* and Before Our New Adventure

Shortly thereafter, Dr. Sangrey lost his mind under mysterious circumstances. At least it seemed so, since he claimed to be living in the past.*

*Read more in the "Interrogation Protocols" - free to download on timmitobbson.com. They are part of the fan package for the book "Legacy of the Inventor".

Following this success, Inspector Hallewell was tasked with bringing down the Guardians' global organization. Since this required the cooperation of nearly every country on Earth, a new special operations group was created: A mixture of police and secret service with far-reaching powers, called UNITE. Working for UNITE, Inspector Hallewell received the new rank and title of *Commissioner*.

Since then, the inventor James Eckles has been living under police protection because he fears another kidnapping by the Guardians. He has also been deeply interested in researching the history of the pirate Lotterlulu.

Our three friends told him about the treasure hunter Sir London, who is considered an expert in this field. Eckles became friends with Sir London and they created the Lotterlulu Foundation, whose goal is to discover more of the pirate's lost treasures. Surely it won't be long before the two can announce their first joint success.

# The Night Before ...

The radio buzzed, then a voice spoke.

"And you're sure?" it crackled. "So far, everything's quiet."

"Oh, he'll come," replied the man on whose table the radio was lying. He was sitting in a large armchair with a curved shape that was probably meant to resemble the tail fin of a whale. Behind thick panes of floor-to-ceiling glass, fish kept swimming through rays of spotlights.

The man was sitting in a room completely surrounded by water. His face was illuminated by screens hanging from the ceiling above him, showing videos from surveillance cameras. He watched them intently.

"Have I ever been wrong, Erik?" the man asked.

"Of course not," Erik replied through the radio. "But I know how important this operation is to you. And there are some circumstances that make me nervous."

"What, then? Tell me."

"He disclosed the location of the *Belle*. You know what that means. He wants the treasure to be found. And with it, the casket," Erik said. His voice sounded nervous. He was not used to criticizing the other man or expressing his doubts. That had been the downfall of many before him. But this project was just too important. The survival of the organization could depend on it.

"I am well aware of what he is up to. If the treasure is indeed found, your team will make sure that the casket is recovered. It will not fall into anyone's hands but ours. Isn't that right, Erik?"

"My men are in position," he replied. "But so far no one has found the treasure chamber. We had already looked for it, as you know, but there is nothing there."

"Don't be a fool, Erik," the man said, sounding a little annoyed. "It exists, and we'll find it eventually."

Using a small lever, he changed the orientation of one of the surveillance cameras. The image showed six small glass vials, standing in a tidy row inside a container. A greenish liquid shimmered in them. The room that could be seen in the background looked like some kind of laboratory.

"Without him realizing it, we were the ones who fed him all the information. He still thinks he is so brilliant and the acquisition of this intel was due to his ingenuity. He has always been arrogant."

The man leaned back in his chair and mentally reflected on it all once again.

*Through us, he knows about the third elixir and where it is on board our ship, the Volante. He even has the construction plans of the Volante and the shift schedule of the guards - and knows where the ship will lie at anchor tonight. He has to come.*

Suddenly, something moved on the screen.

"Do you see that?" asked Erik. "What in the world *is* that?"

The monitor showed a metal spider the size of a hand.

It crawled toward the neatly lined-up glass vials.

"A remote-controlled surprise. I guess he's not coming in person after all," the man said. "Then we'll catch him tomorrow."

His normally calm heartbeat accelerated rapidly as he watched the spider take not one vial, but two, before quickly disappearing with them.

"Two doses" he murmured, leaning back. "So she's still alive, after all."

# The Sunken Treasure Ship

Eyes closed, I floated calmly in the water. From above I felt the warmth of the sun, from below the coolness of the sea. Since my ears were also submerged, I could hear myself breathing. I was completely relaxed. It was simply wonderful here.

*Splash!*

Something plopped into the water right next to me, snapping me out of my daydreams. Startled, I looked around. A diving mask with a snorkel was floating beside me.

"Hey there, daydreamer," Lilli shouted. "You should practice diving instead of just lazing around."

Lilli and Marvin both dangled their feet off the edge of the research vessel that had become our home for the past few days and looked down at me.

I really should practice diving. Because as much as I loved looking at the underwater world through goggles from the surface, I had a hard time breathing with a snorkel. Let alone a scuba tank. That was probably due to my asthma.

"You may want to go down to the wreck sometime, too," Marvin called.

About 20 feet below me lay the wreck of the Belle.

She was once the largest transport ship in the fleet of the pirate Lotterlulu. Her task at that time was not to conquer other ships, but to safely transport captured treasures.

"I just can't breathe through that thing," I replied.

"Quit telling yourself that," Lilli said.

"Try again," Marvin shouted. "You can do it!"

"You're not made of sugar, you won't melt," said Lilli. Then she leaned close to Marvin and said quietly, but loud enough that I could still understand: "He's made of wood. Driftwood. He just floats around endlessly without moving. Like a piece of driftwood."

Marvin looked down at me and tilted his head. He seemed to be seriously considering whether or not I resembled a piece of driftwood.

"Okay already!" I yelled, stretching the diving mask over my face and putting the snorkel's mouthpiece between my teeth.

Marvin smiled and clapped his hands encouragingly.

I sighed.

*Take it easy.*

Slowly, I turned onto my stomach, dunking my face under the water, and looked at the wreck.

All three archaeologists were down there, handling huge hoses that sucked the fine sea sand from the remains of the Belle. This allowed them to gradually uncover the ship without damaging it.

They had not yet found a treasure of gold and jewels. But it had to be somewhere. After all, it was Lotterlulu's treasure ship. The archaeologists were firmly convinced that the Belle's crew regularly brought their cargo ashore and hid it in a secret place.

There was even a legend that said the treasure's hiding place was at the end of an *eternally burning candle*. But there were no candles here and certainly none that burned forever.

One of the divers waved at me. It was Amilia. I thought she was super nice and really smart too.

With another hand gesture, she indicated I should try to dive down to her.

I shook my head.

She shrugged and turned her attention back to the wreck. Today, the three uncovered what they thought was some kind of diving helmet. Early diving helmets were basically metal spheres with small windows made of glass. They were connected by a hose to a boat on the surface. Through this hose, fresh air could be pumped from the top all the way down into the helmet.

*Fresh air!*

The diving helmet had made me think of fresh air. Immediately, I found it harder to breathe again.

*Calm down. Distract yourself.*

I decided to think about Lotterlulu. He was considered very inventive and had become so wealthy, he could employ the best engineers. With their work on the Star Runner, Lotterlulu's own ship, they delivered a technological masterpiece. After we discovered the ship on one of our adventures, it was researched in detail, thrilling scientists around the world, before it was bought by an anonymous collector.

I was delighted when I learned that we would once again be able to witness the discovery of one of Lotterlulu's ships. It had been less than two weeks since James Eckles had called to tell us about the Belle. Since we had helped him a lot in our last adventure, he had invited Lilli, Marvin and me to join the salvage of the wreck for a week. We had had to beg our parents quite a bit for them to let us take this trip. They had agreed only because a team of archaeologists was going to watch over us.

Now I was breathing calmly and evenly again.

The underwater world was truly fascinating. Nowadays, people could explore it quite easily. With scuba tanks and flippers, you felt safe, almost like a fish. Back in Lotterlulu's day, you had to put on a heavy helmet, and walking across the sandy seabed would take all your strength.

Suddenly, a thought occurred to me. I lifted my head out of the water, pulled my goggles and snorkel off my face, and turned to Lilli and Marvin. They were still sitting on the edge of the boat, dangling their legs.

"What would pirates need a diving helmet for anyway?" I called to them.

They looked over to me, but didn't seem to understand. At almost that exact moment, something strange caught my eye.

All three archeologists were diving below me, which should have left no one but Lilli and Marvin on board. But that did not seem to be the case.

Nervously, I called out, "Hey, did one of you get up in the last few minutes?"

Both shook their heads.

What had I noticed?

*Important: To find the solution to the puzzle, you sometimes have to go back some pages. Often the text or the pictures from earlier chapters give important clues. If you get stuck, you will find another clue to each puzzle in the back of the book. The solution is always at the beginning of the next chapter.*

# Genius à la Lotterlulu

"Someone opened the door behind you!" I shouted. Lilli and Marvin wheeled around. But their tense faces relaxed again a moment later.

"Hazelnut!" Marvin called out, "Come here, sweetie!"

A small white and brown dog dashed over to him. He wagged his tail and eagerly tried to lick Marvin's face. Marvin only half-heartedly fought off the licking attacks. He loved the boat dog, as he loved almost all animals, and he didn't seem to mind the odd wet kiss.

"Oh, gross, half your face is wet," laughed Lilli.

"His tongue is really rough," said Marvin.

"He's like your personal washcloth," said Lilli as she stood up. "I'll give you two lovebirds some privacy."

She got a running start and jumped into the sea next to me.

Hazelnut seemed to consider jumping after her, but then decided against it and continued slobbering all over Marvin.

"Are you okay?" asked Lilli, now swimming toward me.

"I just can't breathe well through those things," I said. "It's annoying."

"It'll be fine," Lilli said. "Nobody's forcing you, okay?"

That was nice of her, I thought. The next moment she laughed as she splashed water in my face and briskly swam away.

"Thank you!" I exclaimed. "That was great. Doesn't burn my eyes or anything."

"You are made of sugar after all," she replied.

❖ ❖ ❖

A few hours later, everyone was back on board. We had just finished our lunch and were helping Amilia check the diving equipment. She had already taught us a lot. My job right now was to refill the empty scuba tanks.

Amilia tapped a colored bar built into each tank. "A red bar means the pressure inside is low and the tank is practically empty."

But I hardly listened. All the time I felt as if I had noticed something important today. But what? Mentally, I went through the last few hours again.

"Timmi?" asked Amilia. "Earth to Timmi. Are you with us?"

"I'm sorry," I said. "Now I am."

But that wasn't really true. What had I noticed today? I had to remember.

Amilia put her hand on my chin and turned my face so I was looking into her eyes. "Are you nervous about tomorrow?" she asked me softly. "You've already talked to him on the phone. He's nice."

"Tomorrow?" I whispered, still lost in thought.

"Your meeting with Ruo Tultell. The discoverer of the Belle."

*Oh yes, that's right*, I thought. A little-known researcher named Ruo Tultell had been the first to locate the wreck and had told the Lotterlulu Foundation where it had been found. He had sounded really nice on the phone. But now it dawned on me again what I had noticed earlier today.

"Amilia, what on earth did pirates need a diving helmet for?" I asked.

"I don't know. Maybe to recover a treasure chest that accidentally fell off the ship?"

"Or to hide a treasure," I called out.

Lilli and Marvin paused and looked at me.

"A hiding place under water?" asked Lilli.

"In an underwater cave!" exclaimed Marvin.

"That would be brilliant!" I said. "Genius à la Lotterlulu!"

"Genius à la Lotterlulu," Marvin repeated softly.

I looked over at my friends. We were thinking the same thing.

"Amilia?" I asked. "How does the dinghy work?"

❖ ❖ ❖

"There are lots of caves in the cliff under the water," Lilli said as she resurfaced. She pushed up her diving mask. Her eyes sparkled with excitement. "But I think I know which one we need to look in."

Which cave is the right one?

# The Dive

"Do you remember? According to legend, the treasure chamber is at the end of an eternally burning candle," Lilli said. "There's a pattern in the rocks that looks exactly like a burning candle. The flame starts a little above the surface of the water, directly beneath the hut. And at the very bottom of the candle is a cave opening."

"We'll have to tell the others," Marvin said.

❖ ❖ ❖

"We can't dive today," said Chawla, another archaeologist. "It will be dark soon."

"But we can send the drone in," Amilia said, opening a large box. "It can fly and dive. And everything it sees will be transmitted to us via video."

"Awesome!" said Marvin.

❖ ❖ ❖

A short time later, we all sat enthralled in front of a screen that showed the drone's footage. It was still hovering in the air, roughly where we had been before with the dinghy.

"And dive!" said Amilia, who was doing the piloting.

First, she gently set the drone down on the surface of the water. Then she flicked a switch and the drone slowly sank lower.

"It sucked in a little water to get heavier and sink," Chawla explained. "Underwater, its propellers pull it forward."

"So cool!" said Lilli.

On the screen, we soon saw the entrance to the cave.

"Pretty dark," I whispered.

At the same moment, Amilia pressed a button and the image became brighter. "We aim to please," Amilia said. "Headlights."

The drone dove into the dark tunnel. We recognized rocks and sand. Every now and then we could catch a glimpse of a fish. For a few minutes, we didn't see much more than that.

"This tunnel goes really deep," Lilli said.

"True. The picture is getting worse. I'm dropping a repeater," Amilia said. "They're smaller drones that keep the radio signal up."

The dive continued for a while. Then, suddenly, there was a dead end.

"Is it the end of the tunnel?" I asked.

"There's a cavity above us," Amilia whispered. She moved the drone upward, and all at once it pierced the surface of the water.

"A secret cave!" exclaimed Marvin.

"What's that back there?" I whispered. "The round rock."

"That's a stone slab. A kind of rolling door," said Corey, number three on the team of archaeologists. "When you roll it to the side, you reveal the passageway hidden behind it."

"Unbelievable," said Amilia. "So, then. All the scuba tanks are filled. Tomorrow morning at sunrise, we'll be off."

Marvin clapped his hands and bobbed up and down with excitement. There it was. Our new adventure.

❖ ❖ ❖

When the drone was back and stowed in its box, the sun was already setting. Marvin played with Hazelnut and Lilli watched the sunset colors light up the evening sky. I took the boat binoculars and joined her.

"Pretty, isn't it?" I asked.

"What?" she asked, looking like she had no idea what I was talking about. "Pretty?"

"Yeah, the sunset," I said. "The sky?"

Confused, her eyes turned back to the colorful spectacle. "If you say so," she said.

Sometimes she was really strange. I took the binoculars, brought them to my eyes - and they were instantly snatched away from me.

"Very good," Lilli said, looking through them herself.

"So you *do* like the sunset after all," I said.

"Nonsense," she said, pushing the binoculars back into my hand. "Don't you notice anything? Look at the fishermen!"

 What did Lilli find suspicious?

# A Restless Night

"I think they're just pretending to fish," Lilli said. "Look at the fishing poles: They cast them in the direction they're looking, but the current is bringing the lines under the dock to the other side. They can't even see the little floats attached to their lines that way."

"They wouldn't even notice if a fish was biting," I reasoned. "At least not right away."

"No fisherman fishes like that. Nobody does," whispered Lilli.

"Then who are they?" I asked. "I don't like this at all. Let's go tell Marvin and the others."

After we had shared our suspicions with the others and everyone had made up their own mind by looking through the binoculars, we sat gathered around a table on the dive deck.

"Treasure thieves, probably," Amilia said thoughtfully. She looked worried. "They're waiting for us to find something valuable."

"Now of all times. Who knows what's in the cave," Corey said.

"I'm sure Lotterlulu's treasures are in there," Marvin said. His eyes grew wide. "From years of raids."

"We can't let the treasure thieves get wind of this," Chawla said.

"Mountains full of gold. Sparkling jewels," Marvin fantasized.

"But we can't just sit here," Amilia said. "We have to find out what's behind the stone slab."

"Treasures as far as the eye can see. Piled up to the ceiling," whispered Marvin, quietly clapping his hands.

"So, we'll dive at night. Under cover of darkness," said Corey.

"I don't know," said Chawla. "Let's notify the police."

"The police on these islands aren't always reliable. Not like the police at home," Corey mused.

For a moment, everyone fell silent. Then we looked expectantly at Amilia.

"All right," she said, "tomorrow morning before sunrise we'll set out and see what's behind that rock. All the scuba tanks are filled and the equipment is ready to go."

"Early to bed tonight," Corey said. "The alarm clock rings at four tomorrow."

❖ ❖ ❖

I slept uneasily. In my dreams, I saw Lotterlulu. He looked old and fragile. But most of all, he looked like someone I had seen before. But I couldn't figure out who he reminded me of. Old Lotterlulu shook his head as if to warn me. Then he began to speak, but I could not understand him. No words came out of his mouth, but rather a growl.

Lotterlulu growled like a dog!

I woke bathed in sweat. What a nightmare! I kicked the blanket aside and let the cool night air flow over my body.

Then it growled again. I winced. Was I still dreaming?

*Grrrrrrrrrrrrrrrr!*

That came from my room! From some dark corner!

*Don't move*, I thought to myself. *Breathe quietly. Don't make a sound.*

*GRRRRRRRRRR!*

Slowly, inch by inch, I turned my head to the side to look in the direction of the growl.

"Hazel?" whispered Marvin sleepily. "What's wrong?"

Hazelnut! Of course, it was just Hazelnut. He plodded out of the darkness of his sleeping corner and looked alertly at our cabin door.

❖ 21 ❖

"Something isn't right," Marvin said. "Quiet, Timmi!"

We both stood up without making a sound. Marvin petted Hazelnut and tried to calm him down.

"We have to check," I said, thinking of Lilli. She was sleeping in another cabin. Was she in danger?

Quietly, I opened our door. At first only a crack, through which I peered. Nothing to see, nothing to hear. Suddenly, Hazelnut shot out and ran straight up the stairs.

"Hazelnut, no!" cried Marvin.

But by then our boat dog was already gone. We heard him barking excitedly and then something splashed into the water.

Marvin and I ran after him. When we reached the top, I stepped out into the open. The night was pitch black. Clouds had drawn together and completely blocked out the light of the moon.

Hazelnut dashed toward us, greeting us joyfully. He seemed calm again.

Now Amilia and Lilli appeared. The barking had woken them up.

"I'm afraid we've had an uninvited guest," Amilia said.

"The treasure thieves!" said Marvin.

"We need to check everything," Amilia said. "Everybody, stay close." As we entered the scuba gear room, Amilia paused. "Someone's been in here. But nothing seems to be missing."

"Something is," Marvin said. "Something is different."

 What did the intruder change (other than the water on the floor)?

# Now or Never

"Someone let the air out of the scuba tanks. Amilia, you said earlier that all the tanks were full. The indicator should be green on all of them," Marvin said.

"You're right, Marvin. Good catch," Amilia praised him and tousled his hair.

"But that means they know about our plan to dive before sunrise," Lilli said. "They found out about the cave!"

"So it seems," Amilia said. "But how is that possible?"

"Spies," Marvin whispered.

"Corey, Chawla and I have known each other for years. None of us would ever work with treasure thieves."

"I bet they were listening in on us," Lilli said. "I thought it was funny that one of the fishermen on the dock had headphones on the whole time."

"Yes, exactly," I said. "There was also a cable. That led from the headphones to a tent."

"A directional microphone?" pondered Lilli.

"A directional microphone!" agreed Marvin and I at the same time.

"You can use it to eavesdrop on someone so far away?" asked Amilia. "That could definitely explain it."

She thought for a moment and seemed to come to a decision.

"We need to get going right away," she said, "We'll refill our scuba tanks and I'll dive down with Corey."

"But maybe the thieves are in the cave as we speak," I warned.

"We can take care of ourselves," Amilia said, sounding so determined that I didn't dare disagree.

❖ ❖ ❖

It was still dark when Amilia and Corey approached the tunnel underwater that led into the cliff and up to the cave. Both wore a camera on their forehead that transmitted everything directly to us.

To make the dive as quickly as possible, they each used a Driver Propulsion Vehicle, or DPV for short. As they held on to the device, its motor pulled them briskly forward. Each DPV also had a strong headlight, so that the surroundings were illuminated.

Just like when we watched the drone dive, we sat spellbound in front of the screen and followed the action. On the left, we saw the video from Amilia's camera, and on the right, Corey's. The dark hole of the tunnel entrance appeared in the rock, seeming hazy and unreal. It looked eerie.

"Okay, here we go," Chawla said. "They're going in."

On the monitor, the gloomy hole grew steadily, enveloping them in darkness. Suddenly, they were inside.

On the videos, you could see almost nothing except little white dots that kept darting through black like shooting stars through the night sky.

Every now and then, the rock walls of the tunnel or its sandy floor appeared at the edges of the screen.

Chawla picked up a microphone from the table and spoke into it, "According to the drone's footage, the tunnel is about to go down a steep slope. Watch out."

Amilia and Corey both nodded, confirming that they had understood Chawla. Unfortunately, they could not talk to us while they were diving because they had to breathe through their mouthpieces.

I was nervous. What if the thieves were in the cave? So I got up, grabbed the binoculars and walked to the edge of the ship. From here I had a clear view of the treasure thieves' camp. Since we had been awakened so abruptly, I must have looked through the binoculars at least five times, trying to make out something in the camp.

But the sky was still thick with clouds, making the night too dark to see anything. I sighed.

"They've arrived!" exclaimed Lilli.

I quickly ran to the screen. They made it!

"How's the video feed?" asked Amilia. "Can you see anything?" Just like Corey, she had taken off her mouthpiece and could now talk to us over the radio.

"The image is great," Chawla said. "The repeaters are running fine."

"There's an old diving helmet back there next to the stone slab," Amilia said. You could hear how excited she was. "And a saber!"

"Wow," Corey said. "No one's been here in centuries."

Next to me, Marvin furrowed his brow. There was something he didn't seem to like at all. "Watch out!" he shouted. "The treasure thieves have already been there! Maybe they still are."

 How could Marvin tell that someone must have been in the cave recently?

# The Treasure Chamber

"The big rock on the floor to the left of the diving helmet. It wasn't laying there when the drone was inside," Marvin explained. "It must have fallen down when the treasure thieves rolled the big round stone aside."

Amilia searched the floor with the flashlight. "Yes, you're right. There are tracks here. The stone slab was rolled to the side recently," she said.

"But then they're not inside anymore," Corey said. "They wouldn't have rolled the rock back in place and trapped themselves."

"Okay," Amilia said, thinking. "Shall we go in?"

Corey smiled and gave her a mock bow. "But of course."

Together, the two pushed and pulled on the wooden handles. With a grinding sound, the large stone rolled slowly to the side. Behind it, a dark opening appeared in the rock.

"The treasure chamber," Marvin whispered.

"The treasure chamber," Lilli and I repeated in agreement.

Corey stepped aside. He caught Amilia's eye and made an elaborate flourish toward the opening with his hand, offering Amilia the chance to go in first. She accepted the offer. Our eyes were glued to the video feed of her camera.

Slowly, the glow of her flashlight traveled through the cave. We could hardly believe our eyes.

It was exactly as we had hoped it would be. Boxes piled upon boxes, some of them open, loaded with gold and jewels. There were entire sacks full of gold and silver coins, some of which had burst due to long storage, pouring their contents all across the floor.

We saw precious chandeliers, dishes of the finest porcelain, silver and gold cutlery, jewelry boxes with rings, necklaces and even crowns. In another area were collections of expensive fabrics, rare spices, numerous antique paintings and statues. It was incredible.

But what was *that*?

I reached for the microphone. "Amilia, wait. Please shine the light a little to the left."

"Where exactly?" she asked, panning her flashlight back.

"Stop!" I shouted. "Right there. What's that? A statue?" Now Lilli and Marvin saw it, too.

"We've seen those before!" said Marvin.

We all stared at the screen.

"Yes, an old statue," Amilia said. "Nothing special."

"This is not just any statue," I said. "This is exactly the kind of statue that was in one of Lotterlulu's lairs we found."

"Still, just a statue. Nothing special," Amilia said.

"Is there a cross-shaped opening in the statue?" I asked.

It didn't take Amilia long to find it.

"Yes, here, in the one eye," she whispered. "Wait, here's a kind of key on the floor. Its tip is shaped like a cross."

"No way," Marvin whispered.

We could see Amilia picking up the key and examining it in the beam of her flashlight.

"It's newly made. I mean really new," she said. "There's no way it's from Lotterlulu's time."

I thought hard, trying to make sense of it. Lilli had once been given just such a key by her grandfather.

A really old one, though. It had fit into the cross-shaped hole in a similar statue and had unlocked a secret hiding place.

"Amilia, put the key in the opening and turn it," I said. "Listen carefully. Something may open somewhere."

Amilia did not hesitate. When she turned the key, even I heard a *click*.

"That came from behind me," Amilia said, shining her light on a specific area of the cave wall. As she approached the spot, we saw a small secret compartment carved into the rock. It must have just opened.

"Empty," Amilia said. "But there must have been something here recently. You can clearly see a rectangular outline in the dust. Maybe a jewelry box."

"That was the treasure thieves," I said, my mind racing. "They must have brought the key with them. How could they have known?"

"Good question," Chawla said.

Again I looked through the binoculars. Finally, the clouds had cleared and it was bright enough to see something.

"They're gone!" I shouted. "Up and away with their speedboats. They are powered by electricity, that's why we couldn't hear them when they left."

"But at least we know they have a connection to one of these islands. And I bet that's where they're headed," Lilli said, pointing to the map lying on the table next to us.

 What connection did Lilli see between the thieves and one of the islands?

### CHAPTER 07

# Star Island

"Amilia told me that the three big islands are all of volcanic origin and were named after their shape. I remember that the treasure thieves' boats also had a logo like that which said *Star Island Boat Rental*," Lilli explained. "If the boats are from that island, they might be on their way back there now."

"Maybe," Chawla said. "At least it's a small lead."

"Which island are we meeting Ruo Tultell on?" I asked.

"On Star Island," Chawla replied, smiling. "Today."

❖ ❖ ❖

A few hours later we were sitting in a small and rather rickety yellow seaplane. The ocean glistened as it passed beneath us. I looked out the window, deep in thought:

*How on earth did the treasure thieves know what was in the cave? How could they have found out about the statue and make a key that fit perfectly? It seems they just hadn't known where the entrance to the cave was. And we had solved that mystery for them.*

"We'll find the boats for sure," Marvin interrupted my thoughts. "They're bright red. Hard to overlook."

"But they have more than two hours head-start," I said.

"Star Island Boat Rentals. It shouldn't be hard to find that company," Lilli said. "Chawla talked to Ruo Tultell on the radio. She already told him everything. He wanted to ask around and find out the address."

We had talked to Ruo Tultell on the phone before, but had never met him in person. On the phone, he sounded like a nice grandpa. He told us that he had only succeeded in discovering the Belle because we had found out so much about Lotterlulu in our last adventures. Hopefully he would help us and not get in our way.

❖ ❖ ❖

"So you're Timmi, Lilli and Marvin! I'm so happy to finally meet you," a joyfully smiling man greeted us when we arrived on Star Island.

"Allow me to introduce myself, I'm Ruo Tultell."

We stopped, puzzled. *This* was supposed to be Ruo Tultell?

"Sorry, but we thought you were much older," I said. "Somehow you sounded very different on the phone."

"Oh, really?" he said. "Well, perhaps the connection wasn't the best. The lines here on the islands are getting a little long in the tooth."

"Can we see your ID?" Marvin asked.

"My ID?" Ruo asked, astonished.

"Your passport," Marvin confirmed.

Lilli and I traded surprised glances. But maybe Marvin was right. Better safe than sorry.

"You have to understand, we did have an encounter with treasure thieves last night," I explained.

"So, show us your ID," Marvin persisted with his sternest expression.

"Okay, whatever," Ruo finally said, holding his passport up to Marvin's face.

Marvin took his time with the examination. Again and again, his gaze wandered back and forth between the photo and Ruo.

"You look a lot older here, too," Marvin said.

"You've got to be kidding me," Ruo grumbled, pocketing his passport again. "Besides, I found the boat rental place. Hop in my car and we'll drive there."

"Why didn't you say so in the first place?" asked Marvin reproachfully, marching off.

Ruo gave me a puzzled look and held up his arms as if to silently ask what he had done to deserve being treated like this.

"Sorry," I said meekly, trotting after Marvin.

"Marvin can be a real pain sometimes," Lilli said, grinning. "I'm sure you'll get along great with him. I'm looking forward to that."

❖ ❖ ❖

A few minutes later we reached the boat rental. Quietly, we sneaked around the building until we found a spot with a good view.

"Three speedboats," I mused. "But they're blue."

"Something's wrong," whispered Lilli.

What seemed suspicious to Lilli?

# Hot On the Heels

"The paint on the boats is fresh. Do you see the cat on the dock in front of us? It's licking its paw," said Lilli.

"And it's blue," I said.

"Exactly. There are cat paw prints on the boat on the lower right. I bet the boats have been repainted in a hurry," Lilli said. "There are paint buckets in the dumpsters, too."

At that moment, a motorcycle drove up to the front of the building. "Get down!" hissed Ruo. "And not a sound."

We huddled close to the ground.

"MMM!" mumbled Marvin. There was a mixture of surprise and disgust in his gaze. His finger was stuck in a plant that had closed around it. It seemed as if the plant was sucking on Marvin's finger.

"Ssh," Ruo said.

The motorcyclist was fully dressed in green leather and wearing a helmet. Slowly, he got off his bike.

"MMM!" Marvin moaned again. Gradually, he pulled his finger out of the plant's mouth. It was covered in slime.

Now the driver headed toward the main entrance of the building and disappeared from our field of vision.

"He's gone," I whispered.

"That's *disgusting*!" Marvin complained, looking at his slimy finger.

"Carnivorous plants," Lilli said. "As soon as you touch them, they snap shut."

"Plants that can move!" said Marvin. "How cool is that? And they eat *meat*?"

"Mostly flies. These plants are everywhere on the island. Amilia told me," Lilli said. "Hey, where did Ruo go?"

We looked around and saw him hurrying toward the motorcycle, crouched down. Then he tampered with the bike.

"What's he doing?" asked Lilli.

"Oh no, what if the driver comes back now," whispered Marvin. But Ruo quickly finished and dashed back to us.

"I know who the driver is. A woman named Shila," Ruo said. "I also know who she works for. It's crystal clear who's behind it all."

"Who?" I asked.

"I'll tell you about that later. I bet Shila was sent to pick up the item stolen from the cave and bring it to her employer. We have to go after her."

"But your car won't be able to keep up with this bike," Marvin said. "It'll get away from us."

"It's always served me well," Ruo said, sounding a little offended. "It just has a little trouble going uphill"

"It's a little junky, unfortunately," Marvin commented.

"It's old, but it's far from junk," Ruo said.

"It's about to fall apart. It's covered in rust," Marvin said.

"And your finger is covered in slime," Ruo said.

Marvin looked at his finger, which he had probably forgotten for a moment, with renewed disgust.

"Look out! She's coming back," I whispered.

We ducked and watched Shila, who was now carrying a satchel. The stolen item must have been in there.

She swung onto her motorcycle and sped away. After a few seconds, she was out of sight.

"I owe you an apology," Marvin whispered to Ruo. "That was quite an excellent chase. We almost kept up with her."

"Is Marvin always like this?" asked Ruo.

"He's cheekier than usual," Lilli admitted. "I think he likes you."

"Wonderful," Ruo said, standing up. "Lucky me. Let's go, kids!" We ran to his car and hopped in. Ruo started the engine, which made a loud roar, and drove as fast as he could. It was a rather leisurely pace.

"I sabotaged her oil tank," Ruo said. "Now it has a small hole in it and will keep leaking fluid. As soon as we reach an intersection, we stop and look for oil. Then we'll know which way she went."

"Not a bad plan," I said. "Right, Marvin?"

"Not exactly environmentally-friendly," he grumbled, and folded his arms.

❖ ❖ ❖

The track of the motorcycle led further and further along the steep coast. The roads here spiraled upwards, but Ruo always drove carefully.

At the fifth intersection, we lost the trail.

"She probably doesn't have any more oil in the tank," Ruo said. "She won't get much farther on that bike"

"And now?" I asked. "Which way did she go?"

"From the looks of it, it must be that road," Ruo said.

 Which road did Ruo mean?

# Outsmarted

"She couldn't have taken the path on the far left. She would have destroyed the cobwebs hanging next to the barrier. She couldn't have taken the path on the far right either. Here, her motorcycle would have left tracks in the dirt, just like our car," Ruo explained. "So she must have gone down one of the two middle roads. They're both littered with these carnivorous plants – we know they close up as soon as you touch them. Since only the left of the two middle roads has a lot of the plants closed, I'm pretty sure that's where she drove."

"That's what I was about to say," Marvin agreed.

"Yeah, sure," Ruo said. "I wouldn't have expected anything less."

"Oh really?" said Marvin, smiling.

"No," Ruo said. "Now, everyone, please jump into the cargo bed. I don't want Shila to spot you when we pick her up. Hide under the tarp."

"What exactly are you planning?," I asked.

"Without oil, she can't drive. I'll offer to give her a ride. As much of a hurry as she was in, I'm sure she won't want to stand on the side of the road waiting," Ruo said. "She'll get in and tell me where she wants to go."

"We need to find out what item was stolen from the treasure chamber in the underwater cave. She must have it in her bag," I said.

❖ ❖ ❖

It was terribly stuffy under the tarp. In sharp contrast to the comfortable seats, we were now lying on bare metal. We were getting shaken around hard.

I hoped that it wouldn't be long before we reached Shila. At the same time, I had an uneasy feeling.

"Do you think Shila is dangerous?" I asked Lilli and Marvin.

"She looked pretty cool in her green leather gear," Lilli said. "I think she's tough, a real professional."

"Yes," Marvin said, suddenly sounding excited. "She's part of a big gang of thieves. Who knows - maybe she'll stop at nothing."

I looked into Marvin's big eyes and instantly became even more nervous. He seemed to notice.

"Maybe she's really nice, too," he said.

"Yeah, sure," I whispered.

Suddenly, the car came to a stop.

We heard the door open and Ruo say something.

But under the tarp, we couldn't make out a single word.

"Timmi," Marvin whispered. "Your walkie-talkie. Quick!"

"What? What for?" I asked.

Marvin just waved his hands, which was probably intended to add emphasis to his request.

"I can't reach it," I said. "You have to get it out."

Slowly I turned so that Marvin could reach my backpack. This caused the tarp above us to move just a little.

"Wait," whispered Lilli.

We couldn't let Shila notice we were laying on the cargo bed. Lilli reached out her hand to prop up the tarp.

"Okay," she finally said, nodding at me.

I kept turning until Marvin got to my backpack and fished out the walkie-talkie. At that moment, we heard the passenger door open and someone get in.

"I left my walkie-talkie on the rear seat," Marvin whispered. "I put it on continuous transmission."

He turned on my radio and we could immediately listen in on what was being discussed up front.

"To the port, then," Ruo said. "That's where I need to go, too. May I ask which ship?"

"You may," said a female voice that surely belonged to Shila. She sounded annoyed. "The Volante."

"What a coincidence," Ruo said. "That's my destination, too. I'm expected on the Volante!"

Ruo must have just made that up. What was he planning?

"*You?*" asked Shila. "And why?"

"I'm a professor of history. An expert on pirates."

"Okay, that fits," Shila said, laughing.

"Excuse me?" asked Ruo.

"Well, how you look," Shila said. "Like a professor."

"Is that a compliment?" asked Ruo.

"Take it how you like," Shila said. "Care for a little test?"

"Sure, go ahead," Ruo said.

"What does the name Star Runner mean to you?" asked Shila.

"The Star Runner was the fastest ship of the greatest pirate of all time. It belonged to Lotterlulu," Ruo said. "He was in love with a woman named Maria. She used to ask him to come back home as quickly as possible. Lotterlulu assured her his new ship was so fast, it could fly back to her over the stars."

"Pretty corny," Shila said. "But to my knowledge, the greatest pirate of all time was a man named Riverblood."

"What?" cried Ruo indignantly. "Ridiculous!"

"Really? I'm sure your host will see it differently," Shila said.

"My host?" asked Ruo.

"On the Volante," Shila said.

"Well, in that case, he's clueless," Ruo said.

Right then, the engine of our car started to sputter.

After a few more feet, we came to a stop.

"Give me a break," Shila said.

"This happens all the time," Ruo said. "Come on, you can help me. It'll go faster."

Shila sighed. Then we heard both doors open and shortly thereafter the hood was raised with a squeak. I pulled back the tarp a little. This way, Lilli, Marvin and I could continue to listen in on what was being discussed outside the car.

"Hold the hood for me," Ruo said. "Thanks."

"I can do more than that. I love engines," said Shila.

"Don't worry, I've fixed it many times. It has its little quirks. Please stand next to the car, hot fluid could shoot out any minute," Ruo said. "But please keep holding the hood up, I'll just get my tools."

We heard Ruo run back and get in. Then everything happened very quickly. Suddenly, the engine started and the next moment, the car leaped forward. The gearbox howled and we zoomed off.

"Hey!" Shila shouted as we sped past her. The surprise in her eyes only increased when she saw our heads peeking out from under the tarp.

"She left her bag," Ruo shouted. "We tricked her!" He braked once sharply, causing the hood to fly shut, and then accelerated again, leaving Shila in the dust.

❖ ❖ ❖

Some time later we found ourselves in a busy restaurant near the island's capital. It had observation decks built right on top of the cliff, offering spectacular views. A large number of tourists bustled about here, so we didn't stand out. At least that's what we hoped.

One of the waiters greeted Ruo with a nod, presumably because they knew each other from previous visits, and seated us to a table slightly off to the side.

"Finally! Now we can open the satchel," Lilli said. "I'm bursting with curiosity."

"In a minute," Ruo said. "First I have to let you in on something."

"Let us in?" I asked. "On what?"

"It's all about this guy," Ruo said, tossing a photo of an old, gaunt man onto the table. "This is *him*."

"Who?" asked Lilli.

"The Supreme Guardian of the Dark Power," Ruo said almost thoughtfully. "Their leader."

A shiver ran down my spine. We all stared at the image. The head of all the Guardians. Dr. Sangrey had warned us about him at the end of our last adventure. Ruo Tultell must have learned about the Guardians through his research on Lotterlulu.

"The photo was taken just a few weeks ago," Ruo said.

"And this is his ship, which he calls Volante. It's gigantic."

Ruo tossed a second photo onto the table.

"Wow," I Marvin. "Looks amazing."

That's when I noticed something.

I immediately pushed my chair a little away from Ruo.

"What's the deal here?" I asked.

What was I suddenly worried about?

# The Prisoner

Ruo noticed me staring first at his hand and then at the photograph of the Guardian. Embarrassed, Ruo played with his ring.

"That's right, Timmi," Ruo said. "He's wearing the same ring as me in the photo."

"Why?" I asked. "It can't be a coincidence."

"You're right," Ruo replied. "There is a connection between him and me. It's a long story. And it is time to fill you in."

"It had better be good, or we're out of here," Lilli hissed.

"Is that a Guardian signet ring?" I asked. "Are you one of them, too?"

Ruo sighed deeply. "Look at the ring closely. Don't the three stars remind you of something?"

I was far too upset to think clearly. But he was right. I had seen that symbol somewhere before.

"The three stars," Marvin said. "That's one of Lotterlulu's symbols. Remember the portrait of Lotterlulu in your grandpa's house, Lilli? The three stars on the pirate hat?"

"Right, Marvin," Ruo said, smiling. "So, are you ready to finally discover the truth?"

"Go ahead," I said, taking a puff of my inhaler.

"It all starts with Lotterlulu. At the height of his power, he led numerous pirate ships. There was only one other pirate at that time who was similarly successful. He called himself Riverblood. They were in competition with each other, but sometimes they worked together, too. This was the case when they attacked the treasure ship of the royal fleet one night. A wild firefight broke out between the king's five ships and seven pirate ships. The battle lasted for hours. But in the end, Lotterlulu and Riverblood were victorious. However, the greatest treasure they found aboard the king's ship was not gold. It was a prisoner from a faraway land. He was all skinny from the long captivity and at the end of his strength. Lotterlulu invited him to the captain's cabin to learn more about this strange man. In gratitude for being rescued, he gave Lotterlulu an old book that was among his belongings."

Nervously, I clung to the edge of the table. Was he talking about *the* book?

"On the first page was written El Iksir. It's the same book you've held in your hands once before," Ruo said.

I couldn't believe it. He was actually talking about the book that Lilli, Marvin and I found on our search for the Star Runner. The book that the Guardians wanted to protect at all costs. At that time, we only held it in our hands briefly, before we lost it to the Guardians again.

"Now you will finally learn the book's secret," Ruo continued. "It contains encrypted instructions for creating unbelievably powerful elixirs. The prisoner told Lotterlulu how to decipher one of them. It was the *Elixir of Eternity*. If you took it regularly, you got older, but much, much slower than usual. However, the longer you took it, the more you would notice strange side effects. Things like... changes in the color of the eyes and the color of the mouth. They became..."

"Black," I whispered.

"Black," Ruo confirmed, nodding at me.

"The Guardians of the Dark Power," said Marvin. "They all take the elixir!"

"How old do the Guardians get?" asked Lilli. "How old?"

"If you take it regularly, there seems to be no end to it. At least, I don't know of anyone who died of old age despite taking the elixir," Ruo said.

"Eternal life? No way!" said Lilli.

"That's what Lotterlulu thought at first, too. He doubtless would have wanted to keep the book secret, but unfortunately, it was impossible."

Why couldn't Lotterlulu keep the book a secret?

# Under Observation

"It was Riverblood who had overheard the conversation. Lotterlulu noticed his face reflected in the mirror on the desk. He must have already been sitting in the chair when Lotterlulu and the king's prisoner entered the captain's cabin," Ruo narrated. "Since Riverblood had overheard everything, Lotterlulu had to involve him somehow. Being able to produce the Elixir of Eternity, the two pirates gained powerful allies in the years that followed. After all, who doesn't want to live forever?"

"A fairy tale, nothing more," said Lilli.

"Just wait, that was only the beginning," Ruo said. "Together, Riverblood and Lotterlulu founded the Guardians of the Dark Power. A secret society that would protect the knowledge of El Iksir."

"Wait a minute. Lotterlulu was being chased by the Guardians. He didn't found them," said Lilli.

"You're right. The Guardians and Riverblood eventually opposed Lotterlulu," Ruo said. "But that's another story."

"Another story? In case you don't know, Lotterlulu was my ancestor," Lilli exclaimed, standing up. "Lotterlulu was not one of the Guardians. He certainly didn't found them!"

"In the first years, the Guardians had a noble purpose," Ruo said. "They only sought to protect the book El Iksir. It was Riverblood who turned the Guardians for evil, making them do things that went far beyond their original noble goal."

Lilli looked pale. She fell back into her chair like a limp rag.

"Today, the Guardians are one of the most powerful criminal organizations in the world," Ruo continued. "But together, here and now, we have a chance to put a stop to them."

"But how?" I asked. "Half the world wants to put a stop to the Guardians. What can we do?"

"Listen. Lotterlulu managed to ward off the Guardians because he got his hands on a document that could have harmed their organization. He threatened to publish the document if anything ever happened to him. And that document can bring down the Guardians even today. It still exists. We can and we must get it."

While listening to Ruo, I let my gaze travel over the rest of the café. Something seemed off to me. Something was not right. But what?

"Do you know where it is?" asked Lilli.

"Lotterlulu had the document safely stored. By a bank. Not just any bank, of course. It's a bank only for pirates."

"A bank for pirate treasure," Marvin said. "That's like the coolest bank ever!"

"Today it's almost forgotten, but in Lotterlulu's day, it was a powerful entity. And it works differently than other banks. When a pirate had captured treasure and wanted to deposit it somewhere safe, he turned to the Bank of Pirates. However, this bank did not put all the treasure in just any vault. Otherwise, it would have been robbed straight away," Ruo said. "No, pirate treasures were hidden in secret places. So secret that not even the pirate who had captured the treasure knew the hiding place. This was safer, because if his crew ever had the idea of mutiny, they couldn't force the hiding place out of him."

"Then how did the pirates get their treasure back?" asked Lilli.

"The hiding place was marked on a treasure map. Each map consisted of two parts. The pirate received one part, which he had to hide himself. The other was kept by the bank. Only those in possession of both parts could find the treasure. But the maps were often difficult to decipher. Many a pirate did not make it. As time passed, the bank added requirements and pirates had to solve a series of riddles to earn access to the bank's services. You had to prove yourself worthy."

"I *love* treasure maps!" exclaimed Marvin.

"We already have the first part," Ruo whispered. "Lotterlulu had hidden it in the cave underneath the eternally burning candle."

Ruo reached into the satchel that we had taken from Shila. He drew out a small casket, covered with patterns and symbols.

"It's a puzzle box," Ruo said. "To open it, you have to move the symbols into a certain position."

"It's beautiful," Marvin said, clapping his hands  softly. "And so mysterious. I think I *love* puzzle boxes."

Ruo immediately stowed the casket back into Shila's bag.

"How do you know so much?" asked Lilli. "And now what about the ring you and that Guardian are wearing?"

Ruo was about to answer when I suddenly realized what had seemed so strange to me. "Wait," I whispered. "This is odd. I think we might be being watched."

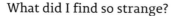

What did I find so strange?

# The Bank of Pirates

"Do you see the woman reading a book at that table?" I asked. "It's a travel guide. They sell them over there at that newsstand we passed earlier."

"I see her," Marvin whispered. "What about her?"

"Well, she's holding the book upside down" I said.

"That's right!" said Marvin. "She's just pretending to read."

"The Guardians have spies all over the island," Ruo said. "Maybe she's one of them. By now, the Guardian Supreme probably knows that we took back the first part of the treasure map - the puzzle box. He'll have his people search for us. And he controls everything here, even the police."

"And where is the second part of the map?" asked Marvin.

"The Bank of Pirates keeps it to this day," Ruo said.

"The bank still exists?" asked Lilli.

"Indeed. But in hiding," Ruo said. "I've already contacted them and asked them to hand over their part."

"But I thought the map was only given to the pirate himself. The one who had asked the bank to hide his treasure," I said.

"Or to his descendants," Ruo said. Then he looked at Lilli.

"Lilli!" I whispered, and got goose bumps. Marvin looked startled, his jaw hanging slack. Lilli glanced nervously between our faces. All our eyes were fixed on her.

"Can you please stop staring at me like that!" she said.

"Lilli," Ruo said. "You are a descendant of Lotterlulu. You are the key to defeating the Guardians of the Dark Power."

"I'm sure I'm not that important," she whispered, avoiding our gaze by staring at her hands.

"You are our only chance," he murmured. "Because you are a descendant of Lotterlulu, the bank will give you the second half of the map."

"How can I prove that we're related?" asked Lilli.

"I've had a report done that proves your relationship to Lotterlulu. Here's a copy for you." Ruo handed Lilli a piece of paper, which she tucked away without reading it.

"You planned all this?" I asked, surprised.

Ruo nodded, then continued, "I've known where the Belle had sunk for a long time, and I also knew that the first part of the map was hidden in the cave of the eternally burning candle."

"But the leader of the Guardians didn't know that," I said.

"Well, he had never found the entrance to the cave. But his people were standing by to secure the puzzle box if the entrance was found," Ruo said. "We have a golden opportunity today to put an end to the Guardians once and for all."

Ruo put his hand on Lilli's forearm.

"Can I count on you?" he asked gently.

Lilli pulled her arm away. She hesitated. Finally, she looked deeply into Ruo's eyes. "How do you explain your signet ring? How did you know about the Belle, the cave, the treasure map?"

"Uh, guys," I said. "She's gone! The woman with the book."

"She's over there!" shouted Marvin. "By the pay phone." Lilli and Ruo didn't seem to hear us at all.

"I will explain everything to you, Lilli," Ruo said. "But there is no time now. Please listen to your instincts. You can trust me."

"The woman keeps squinting over at us," I said.

"I bet she's calling the Guardians," Marvin said.

"We should get out of here," I shouted. "Lilli? Ruo?"

No reaction. Both continued to look deeply into each other's eyes.

"Hello? Let's go!" shouted Marvin, clapping his hands.

Finally, Lilli slowly leaned back. She seemed to have made up her mind. "All right," she said, "I trust you."

Ruo slammed his fist on the table.

"Thank you," he said. "You want to know the meaning of the signet ring? Here, it's a ticket!" Ruo positioned his fist so that his ring fit into a small indentation in the table. Then he turned the ring to the left.

There was a *click*. Now everything happened very quickly.

First, a curtain closed between us and the restaurant. We were instantly hidden from view.

Immediately after, the floor began to spin under our feet. Our table, the chairs we were sitting on, and even the wall behind Ruo - everything whirled around as if on a turntable.

When we came to a stop seconds later, we found ourselves on the other side of the cliff, high up above the sea.

Lilli, Marvin and I had clung desperately to our chairs. Ruo, on the other hand, seemed completely at ease. "Welcome to the Bank of Pirates," he said cheerfully. "Come on, there's a fantastic view." Ruo jumped up and strode to the railing. He took a deep breath of sea air and stretched. But when he looked down at the ocean, he suddenly froze.

"That show-off!" he yelled.

We hurried to him. I could hardly believe my eyes. Deep below us, a man seemed to be standing in the middle of the sea. On the water.

"What?" I whispered. "How is that possible?"

What was he standing on?

◆ 56 ◆

# The Calm Before the Storm

"He's standing on the Volante," Lilli said. "That's an antenna he's holding onto. You could see it in the photo Ruo just showed us."

"A ship that can dive?" I asked in disbelief.

"A ship that can dive," Ruo confirmed.

"I don't believe it," whispered Marvin, visibly impressed.

"A ship for show-offs," Ruo said.

"Is that *him*?" I asked quietly.

"That's him," Ruo said. "Meet the leader of the Guardians. Such a vain peacock of a man."

"But he does look cool," Lilli said.

"That ship is amazing," Marvin said.

"That ship wouldn't stand a chance against the Star Runner," Ruo said. "At least not with Lotterlulu at the helm."

"What?" questioned Marvin. "That's ridiculous."

"How is it ridiculous?" asked Ruo.

"Even if the Volante isn't armed, it's ten times better than the Star Runner," Marvin said. "She could sail right through that old pirate ship."

Ruo now looked downright offended. He raised his index finger as if to lecture Marvin, when someone loudly cleared their throat.

It was coming from somewhere above us. A camera slid out of a recess in the ceiling, moving on a system of rods and rails. Its huge lens made the camera look almost like an eye.

"You have an appointment for the descendant of the pirate Lotterlulu?" asked a voice that seemed to come from the eye.

In a flash, the camera zeroed in on Lilli. It stopped right in front of her face.

"I take it that's her?" the voice asked.

"Why is everyone staring at me today?" grumbled Lilli.

"Right," Ruo said. "That's her."

With a jerk, the eye turned to Ruo. "You have already sent us all the documents and I must say, your research is impeccable. Still, we need to be sure."

The camera whipped around in a flash and focused on Lilli again.

Suddenly, a small arm with a mechanical claw emerged from a flap under the lens and moved toward Lilli's face.

"Hold still, please," the voice said.

"Whoa, no," Lilli said, slapping the arm aside with the back of her hand like a pesky fly.

"I'm sorry, but this has to be done," said the eye. Now the voice sounded a bit annoyed.

Lilli grumbled and let the little arm approach her. It came closer and closer to her face. Then it swerved for her hair, grabbed one and zipped back into the little flap, disappearing in half a second.

"Ouch!" cried Lilli, rubbing the spot where the hair had just been plucked.

"I will return shortly," the voice said, and the camera swiftly retracted into the ceiling.

"What was that all about?" asked Lilli.

"They will analyze your hair," Ruo said. "This will allow them to confirm your genetic relationship to Lotterlulu."

Nervously, he walked to the edge of the rotating wall, where there was a gap barely wide enough to peek through.

I went after him and did the same. On the other side, I could see a table that looked exactly like the one at which we had been sitting. The curtain had been pulled aside again, making it possible to see the café and all the tourists.

"All quiet," Ruo said.

"Too quiet?" I asked.

"The Guardian Supreme knows we're here," Ruo said. "He'll send his henchmen."

I glanced back at Lilli and Marvin. They had been looking out at the ocean, but quickly turned to us.

"He's gone," Lilli said. "So is the Volante."

"What's going on here?" asked Marvin. He bobbed up and down.

"A storm is coming," Ruo said. "The last stand."

I took a breath from my inhaler. *Concentrate*, I told myself. *Think. Stay calm.* I closed my eyes and tried to remember the words Sir London had once said to me. *If you try to solve all your problems at once, you'll be overwhelmed. But if you deal with them one after the other, you've got a good chance of getting through.*

"Why did the Guardians turn against Lotterlulu?" I asked Ruo. "What happened?"

"Lotterlulu and Riverblood each fell in love," he answered. "Unfortunately, they both loved the same woman. Neither had felt anything like it before, and would not again. But the woman chose Lotterlulu. Riverblood couldn't accept this, and he gave her a poison that put her into an eternal sleep."

Lilli and Marvin came over to us. We all listened to Ruo, fascinated.

"Lotterlulu and Riverblood became enemies. Lotterlulu gave up his life as a pirate to tend to his sleeping love. He found ways to give her food and drink while she slept. The years passed, but she never woke up. Her name was Anna Maria, but he always called her Maria."

Suddenly, Ruo sounded pensive.

"At some point, Riverblood learned she was still alive. And he decided to capture her."

Ruo slumped down on a chair at the table. We sat around him. He took a deep breath and continued.

"It was September 26. The date consisted of Riverblood's lucky numbers, two, six and nine. It was already night when he landed with two ships on the island where Lotterlulu was caring for Maria. Riverblood was intent on taking Lotterlulu by surprise. He had the lights on the ships put out so that they couldn't be seen. A whole troop of 30 pirates disembarked, all with socks over their boots so they wouldn't make a sound."

Ruo uneasily rocked back and forth on the chair. It was as if the story affected him personally.

"Riverblood and his henchmen took their time. He knew he couldn't simply enter through the large metal garden gate with its sharp spikes.

Its creaking would be heard, and Lotterlulu might somehow escape with Maria. Riverblood knew that Lotterlulu had had secret escape tunnels built. No, they had to be absolutely silent so Lotterlulu wouldn't have a chance."

Ruo paused for a moment and smiled mischievously.

"So Riverblood decided to cut a path through the hedge that had been planted around the house. A dark hedge, thick and poisonous. Riverblood's blade cut through it like a hot knife through butter. Without the slightest sound. Riverblood was sure Lotterlulu would not notice his arrival."

"But he was wrong," I guessed.

"When he burst through the door, Lotterlulu and Maria had indeed disappeared. The bed was still warm. They had left only a few minutes ago. Somehow, Lotterlulu must have learned of Riverblood's arrival after all."

"What happened to them next?" Lilli asked.

"Lotterlulu disappeared to a secluded island, hidden and unknown to the outside world. Eventually, Lotterlulu had to give her the Elixir of Eternity, so she wouldn't die of old age. Riverblood has not been able to track them down ever since."

"Ever since?" I asked, confused.

"He must have been searching for her for a long time," Ruo said, playing with his signet ring again.

"But how did Lotterlulu know Riverblood and his pirates were coming?" asked Marvin.

 How was Lotterlulu warned?

 **BONUS QUESTION** Where was the secret passage?

# Attack of the Guardians

"Lotterlulu had the entire garden and even the hedge strung with fine threads. These led into the house, and little bells hung from their ends," Ruo said. "When Riverblood cut the hedge, one of the little bells fell down. Lotterlulu was warned and was able to escape through a trap door in the floor that led into a secret tunnel, carrying Maria in his arms. Riverblood probably only discovered the hidden entrance because Lotterlulu accidentally caught the corner of the blanket in it."

While Ruo was telling us this, he stood up and peered through the crack again. "They're here!" he said, suddenly frantic. "That was too fast. We're trapped!"

We all sprung to the wall, trying to get a look for ourselves. We couldn't see much, but everyone seemed to be in an uproar. They were running back and forth, and we heard some people calling out loudly.

Suddenly, right at the other side of the crack, a face with a wide, unblinking eye appeared and stared at me. Startled, I fell back and dropped down into one of the chairs.

All of a sudden, the wall in front of us jerkily moved back a little. The turntable under our feet shook, too. Someone was trying to force the rotating wall open.

Thinking quickly, Lilli grabbed one of the old torch brackets from the wall, stuck it in the crack, and shoved against it. Marvin leaped to her side and pushed, too.

"Hey," Ruo yelled toward the ceiling. "We have a problem."

Then he joined in, grabbing the other torch holder and jamming it into the gap.

The rotating wall and floor jolted again. I dove under the spot in the ceiling where the camera had emerged.

"Hello!" I yelled. "They're about to break in."

Something went *thrumm*. Everything around us vibrated. The crack opened an inch. Lilli and Marvin screamed.

"They're breaching the wall!" I yelled. "We need help!"

Just then, the camera whizzed out of the ceiling. It gripped a yellowed envelope in its little claw.

"Here you go," it said. "The second part of the treasure map."

I grabbed the envelope and hurried to help the others.

"We need an extraction," Ruo yelled. No matter how hard we pushed, the crack kept slowly opening.

"You certainly are in a difficult situation," said the eye. "But it's been decades since the last extraction protocol was executed."

"Doesn't matter, do it already!" Ruo cried out.

"An extraction must be earned. Do you see the levers on the wall? They are arranged in a shape that resembles a donkey. You must find and pull the lever that rotates the donkey. Then the extraction will begin. But choose the wrong one, and you are lost."

"You must be joking," Ruo ground out.

"This is the Bank of Pirates. We never joke," said the eye. "Solve the puzzle. Prove yourself worthy of an extraction. And remember, only one lever may be pulled. It must make the donkey rotate."

Without any hesitation, the eye vanished into the ceiling.

"You've got to be kidding me," Ruo groaned.

We all continued to fight hard, trying to stop the wall from turning. However, none of us could really look at the collection of levers, let alone think clearly enough to solve the puzzle.

"Marvin," Lilli grated out. "Stop pushing. You have to solve the puzzle."

"Why me?" groaned Marvin.

"There's an animal in it," Lilli hissed. "Your thing."

"Right. You're right," Marvin said, and let go. He took a few deep breaths as he approached the puzzle, eyeing it thoughtfully. "The levers form a shape that really looks a little like a donkey. The bar in the upper right corner is its head. But which lever is supposed to rotate something?"

Marvin walked up close.

"There are no fingerprints or anything here," he said. "No scratches. I don't think the metal plate can be moved at all. It's mounted firmly to the wall."

"Think, Marvin," I groaned. "Think."

Suddenly, something from the other side of the wall banged against the torch holder that Lilli had jammed into the gap. It immediately flew out of our hands and clattered across the floor.

"Marvin!" screamed Lilli. "It's now or never!"

"This one!" shouted Marvin, pulling a lever.

 Which lever was the right one?

# The Escape

Marvin turned the lever next to the inscription "III". As a result, the donkey had turned without anything else moving except the lever. (*First, the donkey seems to be facing to the right. After turning the lever, tilt your head to the right. Now the donkey seems to face to the left.*)

Marvin looked proudly at the result, clapping his hands.

A second later, everything around us started vibrating. Lilli and I screamed as we continued to push against the steadily opening wall. Marvin held fast to the lever that he had just turned and looked up at the ceiling in fear. White sand and little pebbles were trickling down from it. *What was that, an earthquake?*

We could hardly believe our eyes when the huge basalt column that bordered the room to the left suddenly split in the middle with a thunderous roar. Like an elevator, the lower part slowly started to descend, shaking violently, creating an opening.

It wasn't the only one. The adjoining column started to split as well, and the ones after it, too. As they opened, they created a passageway that led through the columns and along the cliff.

"Get in! Go!" yelled Ruo, "I'll try to hold them off."

"In *there*?" Lilli cried.

"That's the extraction route," Ruo shouted. "Now go!"

*This was just plain crazy!*

My gaze searched for Marvin. He looked at me with wide eyes, unable to move.

I felt the wall behind me opening further and further. My feet slid across the dusty floor.

I looked at the passageway. The lower part of the column was no longer moving; the separation was complete. This mighty procedure, which shook the whole cliffside, had caused large cracks in the walls. Small chunks continued to fall here and there. White dust hung in the air.

But the passageway looked stable.

"Lilli," I burst out. "On three!"

Beads of sweat ran down her forehead. She nodded and grabbed Shila's satchel, which contained the puzzle box.

"One... two... three!"

Lilli rushed to Marvin first, grabbed him by the wrist, and pulled him into the passage with her.

"Timmi!" called Ruo. He threw me a necklace that he had pulled up over his head.

"Take this. Take good care of it!" he said, forcing a smile. "It's a matter of life or death."

Without understanding what he meant, I nodded and ran.

Behind us, we could hear Ruo groan as he tried to stop the relentlessly turning wall all by himself.

Quickly, we ran from column to column. We had to watch every step we took, as chunks of rock had chipped off here and there, leaving the ground full of holes, cracks and tripping hazards. One false step, and we would fall into the depths.

After about a hundred feet, we reached the end of the passageway. There was yet another surprise waiting for us.

"The door is locked!" Lilli cried. She rattled and pulled hard on the knob. "See the keys? I bet one of them will fit."

I glanced back at Ruo. He was surrounded by three other people. Now he was holding his hands up. And then there was a woman. She had flaming red hair.

"Shila!" I cried out. "She's with Ruo!"

She stared over at us, but didn't move from the spot. Did she think we were trapped?

"Hey, which key?" shouted Marvin.

I turned to the puzzle and tried to concentrate.

"Are we supposed to try them all?" hissed Lilli.

"I have it," I said. "It must be this one."

Shila saw me pointing at the key. That must have changed her assessment of the situation. She immediately ran toward us.

Which key was the right one?

# Deep Inside the Cliffs

In my mind's eye, I had connected the number-shaped keys with lines. One line went from key one to key two. The next line went from key two to key three, and so on. Finally, the lines formed an arrow, which clearly pointed at the one key in the upper right corner.

As soon as we had fished the key from the wall, everything around us started vibrating just like before. Small pieces of stone fell from the ceiling.

"The passage is closing again!" Marvin screamed.

I glanced at Shila, who had stopped in surprise and was trying to keep her balance on the shaking ground. Marvin was right, the basalt columns that formed the ceiling of the escape route were now descending.

Shila looked over at us. She had immediately understood what that meant. If she didn't reach us in time, she would have to jump down into the sea. Instantly, she ran toward us again. She seemed to fly over the shaking ground.

Nervously, I fumbled the key into the lock.

"Quickly," yelled Lilli.

I breathed a sigh of relief as the door unlocked. We heaved it open, rushed through, and slammed it shut behind us.

With a loud bang, Shila threw herself against the door. But she had no chance. She couldn't get through.

I bent down and peered through the keyhole.

Shila stood on the edge of the cliff and looked down at the sea. She took a few steps back, started to run, and leaped into the depths. She seemed completely relaxed to me. As though there was nothing to it.

I imagined her casually plunging into the brilliant blue water below.

Then a shadow darkened everything on the other side of the keyhole until all I saw was black. The vibrations also came to a halt.

"The passageway has closed," I said quietly. "Shila jumped."

I must have sounded a little worried. At least, Lilli looked at me and said: "I'm sure she made it."

"Definitely," said Marvin, and let himself slowly sink to the floor. Lilli and I did the same. All three of us were completely exhausted.

"Oh no!" I said. "I lost my walkie-talkie. It must have fallen off the table when we were spinning into the Bank of Pirates."

"Not good," Marvin said. "But Lilli and I still have ours. You just can't go marching off without us."

"I wasn't planning to," I murmured, digging a flashlight out of my backpack. I flicked it on and shone its beam into the darkness. Before us stretched a long tunnel that must have been painstakingly carved out of the rock ages ago. It was impossible to see where it led.

For a few minutes we just sat on the ground and tried to regain our strength.

"What was it that Ruo gave you?" Lilli asked. "He said something about *life and death*, didn't he?"

Only then did I remember the envelope and the necklace I was still clutching in my hands.

"A matter of life or death," I answered. "That's what he called it."

I held up the chain and illuminated the pendant with my flashlight. It was a small glass vial, no bigger than my little finger. Inside was a shimmering greenish liquid.

"Could that be one of the elixirs?" I wondered. "But how did Ruo get his hands on it?"

"Ruo is full of secrets, it seems to me," said Lilli.

"They captured him," whispered Marvin.

"Yes," said Lilli. "Let's go. Ruo needs us."

We got back on our feet and dusted off our hands. Lilli and Marvin took out their flashlights, shining them into the darkness that lay ahead of us.

"Then let's get going," I said. "We have to get out of here, find those hidden documents, stop the Guardians, and free Ruo."

"Child's play," said Lilli.

I put on Ruo's necklace and gave Lilli the envelope. "I think this is for you, little pirate's daughter."

"What do you mean, little?" laughed Lilli, and started walking.

"Oh, yeah," said Marvin. "Pirate Lilli. Also known as Piratelli."

"Quiet, Marvin," said Lilli.

"Or Lotterlilli," muttered Marvin. "Lotillilu. Lillilulu."

"Why do you always have to get cheeky when we're exploring dark tunnels?" sighed Lilli.

"That's not true," said Marvin. "I'm cheeky in broad daylight, too."

"I stand corrected," laughed Lilli.

"Piratulli."

"Oh, hush!"

Cautiously we moved forward until a dome finally opened in front of us. On the opposite side, we could see three archways, each leading into a passageway.

"A fork in the road," I said. "But which way leads out?"

"Wow!" said Marvin. "Look over there."

His flashlight illuminated the wall on the left side. Instinctively, I took a step back and felt the hair on the back of my neck stand up. What on earth was hanging there?

It looked like an old pirate. A pirate lurking in the darkness, waiting for prey. His clothes were half rotten and hung from him in rags.

"He's made of wood," said Marvin. "So cool."

"Creepy," Lilli said.

"There's some writing," said Marvin, shining his light on a metal plate strapped to the pirate's chest like armor. He read aloud:

"A ship sails slow if the wind doesn't blow.
Like a good friend, it will show you the way,
But a lull will lead to your final day.
A flame is bidden to show what's hidden."

"Doesn't sound very inviting," I whispered. "Two of the paths must lead to traps."

"Look," said Lilli, pointing to a crate full of candles. Next to it stood a device with a wheel-shaped stone hanging in the center. "The rhyme mentions a flame. That must be a reference to these candles. And that machine is probably some kind of old lighter."

"That thing?" asked Marvin. "Awesome!"

"Does this still work?" murmured Lilli, and spun the stone wheel. Sparks flew through the darkness.

"Wow," I said. "That's really cool."

Lilli took one of the candles and held it close to the sparks. It took a while, but the wick finally ignited.

"You did it!" said Marvin, immediately holding another candle to Lilli's flame.

I did the same, and soon we each held a lit candle in our hands.

"And now?" asked Lilli. "Is something supposed to happen?"

"The riddle mentions wind," I said. "But I don't feel any."

"It also says we need the flame to discover something. Are there any hidden symbols here, maybe?" asked Lilli. "Let's search the archways."

Each of us took one of the three entrances. Inch by inch, we searched the stones for more clues by the light of our candles.

"Wait a second," I said a moment later. "I think I've got it!"

How did I find the solution, and which path was it?

### CHAPTER 17

# A Casket Full of Puzzles

My candle flickered slightly as I held it in the passageway in front of me, while the flames of the other two candles stood almost still.

"Like a good friend, it will show you the way, but a lull will lead to your final day," I repeated the riddle.

"A flame is bidden to show what's hidden," whispered Marvin. "That must be it."

"Yes, there must be an exit somewhere back there," said Lilli. "Otherwise, there couldn't be a draft."

We followed the middle path. It took quite a while until we finally arrived at its end. Before us lay a wall of loosely piled stones. Sunlight shone through the cracks. We could hardly wait to get out. Hastily, we removed the stones and found a thick layer of ivy on the other side. But it wasn't long before we had overcome this last obstacle and literally burst out into the open.

Before us lay a small garden that belonged to an old, seemingly abandoned house. Unsure whether anyone had noticed us, we sneaked over to a rusty garden gate. We scurried through it and arrived in a narrow alley lined with old, but better maintained houses.

"We did it," I said with relief.

"If I'm not completely disoriented, we're in the island's capital," said Lilli. "Let's find somewhere quiet and come up with a plan."

"We should be careful," whispered Marvin. "I bet the Guardians are searching everywhere for us."

"Maybe Latin?" murmu... / Carefully, he touche... / plates under the... / little wheel...

The sun beat dow... streets. Finally, we fou... olive tree. Here, we had...

"Okay," said Lilli. "We... envelope from the Bank o... cave of the eternally burni... should be able to find out wh...

"And take down the Guard.

Lilli took the puzzle box out... a little closer to take a look a... ...ully decorated. Many mysterious sym... ...oned on little square plates.

"Look," Marvin said. He slid one of the plates left, to the edge. "You can move the symbols around."

"You can rearrange them. I bet if we position them correctly, the box will open," I whispered.

"The big half moon can't be moved," said Marvin.

"So many symbols," said Lilli worriedly. "So many possibilities."

"Ruo said that only the pirate himself could decode the treasure map," I reflected.

Suddenly, Lilli's face lit up. "Wait. Look. There are stars here. And this moon! Just like it was back then! Lotterlulu's hiding place in my grandpa's house!"

"That's right," I grinned. "The moon under a tent of stars."

She quickly arranged the symbols so that all the stars were on the edges. All of a sudden it clicked and the casket opened a crack.

We held our breath. Lilli pushed the lid aside. The bottom of the casket was also covered in symbols. There was something written next to them.

"What language is that?" I asked.

ed Marvin. "Can we move them, too?"

the symbols. "Look, the flower-shaped
golden symbols can be rotated clockwise. Like
or cogs."

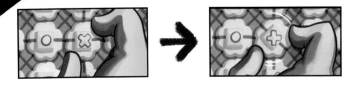

"Okay, on each of these... wheels, there's also a line. It runs underneath the square plate with the symbol," Lilli mused. "And on the bottom of the box, there's a whole web of lines."

"Let's open the envelope from the Bank of Pirates," I said.

Lilli broke the red wax seal and carefully pulled out a yellowed piece of cloth. It showed four figures, each raising up a staff with a symbol.

"Good," said Lilli. "That's the second part of the treasure map. Put them together, and they must make some kind of sense."

My gaze wandered back and forth between the cloth and the box.

"You can turn each wheel so that the line on it is continued by a line on the bottom. That way you can draw a line from each wheel to the next, connecting their symbols," I said. "Like on the cloth."

"I think you're right. And those Latin words might stand for certain places," Lilli mused. "I think we need to find out which is the correct one."

"I think I know the answer," said Marvin.

Which word was the solution?

# Protect and Serve

The figures on the fabric showed which symbols inside the box should be connected by the lines on the wheels.

"The stars have to be connected to the two circles and the diamond to the Y," Marvin said.

"Okay, let's rotate the wheels," Lilli said. "We align the lines on the wheels with the lines on the bottom so that there is a connection between the symbols."

"I bet it will make a pattern that matches one of the symbols next to the Latin words," Marvin said.

"You don't need to turn them. I can see they will. It's the pattern next to *Fons Tutelae*," I said. "But what does Fons Tutelae mean? Or could it be the name of a place?"

"Ruo would know," Lilli said.

"You know who else might?" exclaimed Marvin. "Sir London! We could call him. I have his number."

Marvin excitedly rummaged through his belt pouch and pulled out a small, tattered writing pad.

"Does anyone have any coins?"

❖ ❖ ❖

Shortly thereafter, we all stood close together, listening at the receiver of a public pay phone. I was glad to hear the familiar voice of Sir London.

"Kids! It's good to hear from you," he said. "Are you on the research vessel? The connection is pretty bad."

We quickly told him what had happened - about the cave of the eternally burning candle, about Ruo, about the leader of the

Guardians, the Elixir of Eternity and the hidden documents that we needed his help to discover.

"Fons Tutelae," mused Sir London. "It means something like well of protection or source of protection."

"Anything else?" I asked. "We're a bit stuck."

"Yes, there is," Sir London said. "The island you are on was once considered a hub for pirates. Legend has it that there was a huge cave on this island in which several pirate ships could take shelter at the same time. Imagine a proper harbor with three, four, or maybe even five ships, all in a cave that could be entered directly from the sea. But it is unclear whether this hidden harbor ever really existed. At least, it has never been found."

"But if pirate ships could sail into it, the entrance must have been gigantic," Marvin said.

"Well, maybe it's just a legend," Sir London continued. "In any case, it was said that the cave could also be reached from land, through secret underground passages. The entrance to one such tunnel was known as Fons Tutelae. So in short, you are searching for an entrance to an underground pirate harbor that has been kept a secret for centuries."

"And we don't have any other clues," I said.

"You mentioned that the name Fons Tutelae was next to a symbol. What does that look like? Maybe it stands for a building, or something like that."

We described the symbol to Sir London.

"Wait, I think I have something here," he said. We heard paper rustling. He was probably paging through a book.

"Here it is! There's an old marketplace in the city. In the middle stands a fountain. Its outline resembles your symbol."

*That has to be it*, I thought.

"But listen, children, this is too dangerous," Sir London said. "Please call the police!"

"Ruo told us not to trust anyone," I explained. "The Guardians have the entire island under their control."

"But maybe you could inform Commissioner Hallewell?" suggested Lilli. "After all, she's leading the UNITE special forces in the search for the Guardians. We know her, and if you mention us, they'll put you through to her."

"That's an excell-," we heard Sir London say, when the phone line suddenly crackled and he was cut off in mid-word.

"Hello?" I called out. "Sir London?"

"That happens here sometimes," said someone behind us.

Startled, we spun around.

It was a police officer.

"Then the whole neighborhood has no electricity," he said. "But it'll only be a few minutes, and then you can get back on the phone. Just wait a minute, and I'll keep you company."

The police officer murmured something into his radio.

"I don't think the power is out in the whole neighborhood, though," Marvin whispered. "I think someone cut our connection. We should get out of here."

How could Marvin tell that the electricity wasn't out everywhere?

# The Code

The keypad of the pay phone was still illuminated. The policeman's claim that the power had failed could not be true. Had the telephone connection been interrupted by someone who had been listening in? Could the police have even traced our location through the call?

"No problem," said Lilli. "We were done anyway."

With a determined stride, she walked past the officer and down the stairs, followed by Marvin and me.

"Hey, wait!" said the police officer.

"No time," said Lilli, and kept going unfazed.

"Stop at once!" yelled the officer.

"Go!" I hissed, and we ran as hard as we could.

"Stop! Freeze!" he yelled, and took up pursuit.

Down below, we rushed past the clothing store and into the adjacent alley. It curved so sharply that we couldn't see where it would eventually lead us.

Suddenly, we almost bumped into a truck that had been maneuvered out of a narrow driveway. The engine was running, but the driver was nowhere to be seen.

"Wait," I gasped, looking around.

The police officer was not yet in sight, but his footsteps echoed through the alley. It would only be seconds before he appeared in our line of sight. I tugged on the handle of the truck's passenger door. It opened. "A perfect hiding place," I whispered.

Hastily, we climbed in, closed the door behind, and ducked down.

Shortly afterward, the officer came to a stop right next to the truck. Had he seen us?

We heard him say something into his radio. Then he ran further down the alley.

"That was a close one," I whispered.

❖ ❖ ❖

About half an hour later, we were standing in front of the fountain. We had asked for directions from the most friendly, trustworthy-looking people we could find - and who appeared to know the city. On our way, we avoided large public squares, walked in the shadows, and chose narrow alleys over wide streets.

The fountain really did resemble the symbol from the puzzle box. Four large tentacles of an octopus poked up into the sky like lances, and in between them posed a proud pirate, surrounded by treasures. A large shield was emblazoned in the center.

"Wow, what a giant octopus!" said Marvin.

"We have to hurry," I said. "If one of the people searching for us comes by here, we're done for."

"There must be a secret entrance," Lilli mused. "And I bet the shield has something to do with it."

"Yeah, those are pressure plates," Marvin said, pressing his hand against one of them. It gave way with a squeak.

"Look!" said Lilli. "There's something written on the edge of the shield."

The short message read:

FROM A TO G

"We probably have to push the plates in the right order," I said.

"There are seven letters from A to G. And there are seven symbols on the shield," Marvin pondered.

"But what next?" asked Lilli.

"No idea. Maybe there are more messages hidden on the statue," I said, looking up to the pirate. The sun burned down from the sky relentlessly, making me squint.

"And maybe..." Marvin said, taking out the puzzle box. "Earlier, you said we didn't need to turn the little wheels, because we could recognize the right pattern anyway. But they must be good for something."

We sat under the statue and Marvin began to turn the wheels, arranging the lines to form the pattern for Fons Tutelae. Before he turned the last wheel, he stopped and looked at us expectantly.

"Do it!" hissed Lilli, taking Marvin's hand and turning it.

There was a *click*. The metallic ornaments on the two longer sides of the box fell to the ground with a clatter.

"I'm a genius!" said Marvin. "Here's our code!"

On the two opposing sides of the box, we could now see a row of symbols that had previously been hidden.

There was also a short text written beneath the symbols.

"Put together what belongs together," I read aloud.

"Strange, none of these symbols are on the shield," said Lilli. "They don't match."

"But this must tell us the sequence for the shield," said Marvin. "Come on, let's think."

 What was the code?

Left side of the casket:

Right side of the casket:

**WHAT BELONGS TOGETHER**

# Descent Into Darkness

We followed the hint *"Put together what belongs together,"* and mentally placed the symbols from the two opposing sides of the box on top of each other, causing them to merge into a new set of letters and symbols. *(You can also close the two previous book pages and look through them from page 87 - it is best to hold the pages against a bright light).* The new row showed letters, each followed by one of the symbols also found on the shield. The letters gave the sequence – from A to G. We pushed the plates on the shield in that order.

We immediately heard a dull, booming sound from inside the statue, as if someone had thrown a heavy weight onto the ground. In that moment, the shield sunk down a little. We looked around nervously. There was a flurry of activity in the shadows of the surrounding houses, but no one seemed to have noticed anything.

My fingers trembling with excitement, I grabbed the right edge of the shield and pulled.

It moved.

I paused and let my gaze wander once more. We had to wait for the right moment to sneak through the secret entrance without being seen.

"Flashlights," I whispered.

Lilli and Marvin discreetly held them poised.

"Ready?" I asked and they both nodded. "Then let's go." I pulled the shield open, just wide enough. One after another, we darted inside.

We found ourselves in a very small space. The air was hot and stuffy, and had a musty smell. There was a three-foot-wide hollow in the middle of the pedestal, with a metal pole leading from the ceiling down into the darkness.

I grabbed the rusty safety railing that surrounded the hole and pointed my flashlight down. Its beam didn't reach the bottom.

Lilli wiggled the pole, testing its strength. "It's just like the poles at fire departments," she said. "I always wanted to try sliding down one."

"Well, then," I said. "After you."

Marvin picked up a small rock and threw it into the hole.

"One thousand one, one thousand two, one thousand three."

*Clack!*

"About three seconds," Marvin whispered, his eyes wide. "That must be more than hundred feet."

I didn't even want to question whether Marvin was right or not. Either way, it was deep.

"We're going to need this," said Lilli, and shone her light on an old rope winch hanging from the ceiling. "For safety."

I wasn't entirely happy with the idea of descending into a dark hole, but Lilli was determined. Shortly afterward, we had the rope tied around her. Lilli clenched her flashlight between her teeth, tried to wobble the pole again, and tugged on the safety rope. Everything seemed to be stable.

"See you one the other side," I whispered.

Lilli nodded briefly and then jumped on to the pole.

She slid into the darkness, while Marvin and I operated the winch. The light from Lilli's flashlight quickly got smaller and smaller.

And then it disappeared entirely.

"Oh wow, that's deep," I said.

A moment later, the tension on the safety rope eased abruptly.

"Hey, everyone!" I heard Lilli call. I sighed in relief. She shone her flashlight up at us. "You have to see this!"

Marvin was next, and I went last. We had figured out how to adjust the winch so that it would automatically lock if I slipped off the pole. This made my descent reasonably safe, too.

When I reached the bottom, Lilli and Marvin were standing a few feet away, with their backs to me. They seemed completely fascinated by something in front of them.

"Hey, what's going on?" I asked, hectically trying to free myself from the safety rope as quickly as possible.

"You won't believe this," Lilli stammered.

Marvin turned around and shouted, "Timmi, this is absolutely awesome. Come here! Come here!"

As soon as I was loose, I ran over to them. And it really was hard to believe.

A huge cave stretched out before us, shrouded in a ghostly light. We looked at the roofs of countless old houses that had been built stretching high up the cave walls. Between them ran a maze of stairways and small alleys. Finally, behind the buildings, the masts of abandoned pirate ships rose upwards.

"The cave harbor," I whispered. "We found it."

"Wow, it's incredible!" Marvin said.

"I bet no one's been here in hundreds of years," I said.

"Wrong," said Lilli. "Completely wrong."

Find a clue that confirms Lilli's statement.

 Find all three clues.

# The Needle in the Haystack

"There's smoke coming out of a chimney down there," Lilli said. "And look high up, to the left. There's a satellite dish mounted on that balcony. And look at the rock next to us: a power box."

"That must mean we're not alone down here," whispered Marvin. "That's not good."

"Yep, we have to be on our guard," said Lilli.

An uneasy feeling crept over me. The cave in front of us was massive. How could we possibly find the hidden documents? We needed another clue.

"Marvin, is there anything else on the puzzle box?" I asked. "Did we miss anything?"

"I don't think so," he said, pulling it out of Shila's satchel. We turned and rotated the richly decorated casket, examining it carefully. Nothing. Suddenly Marvin's face brightened. "Wait a minute!" he said, reaching into the satchel again. Then he pulled out four small metal shapes. "These fell off earlier, remember?"

We looked at them in the glow of our flashlights.

"Check this out," Marvin said. He carefully placed one of the pieces over the other and pressed them together. There was a soft *click*. Then he added the third and finally the fourth.

"It looks like a ninja star!" said Marvin excitedly.

"Pirate ninjas?" asked Lilli, giggling.

"I'm just saying it looks like one," Marvin said, sounding a little disappointed. "I get it, there is no such thing as pirate ninjas."

Then his mood picked up again and he said: "Anyway, that's a sign to look out for. Like an X that marks the spot."

I gazed down into the huge cavern. "Guys, we are looking for a needle in a haystack," I said. "And we have no idea who's prowling about down there."

"Or how many," Marvin whispered.

"Ruo needs us," Lilli said. "Remember?"

"Sir London must have notified Commissioner Hallewell. She and her special unit can be anywhere in the world in no time. I'm sure they'll arrive soon," I said.

Lilli looked at me with a mixture of annoyance and disappointment. "You know what, Timmi? Why don't you just climb back up again?"

Then she turned her back on me and went toward the steps that led below.

"Come on, Marvin, let's go," she said.

Marvin gave me an uncertain look and shrugged his shoulders. Then he trotted after her.

I gazed back at the pole I had just slid down. No way I could climb it all the way back up. I rolled my eyes, sighed, and followed my two friends.

❖ ❖ ❖

We sneaked through ancient, winding alleys. They must have been full of life once, but now were shrouded in an eerie silence. Everything gave me the impression that the houses had been abandoned in a hurry.

Again and again, there were objects on the ground: sabers, bags, even coins. One table still had plates and cups on it. A few steps farther, I recognized the derelict skeleton of a horse-drawn carriage. So there must have been horses down here once. I couldn't stop marveling.

And finally, we reached the harbor.

In front of us loomed the remains of four genuine pirate ships. Even in a state of partial collapse, they still looked proud and powerful. Real cannonballs, old barrels, and weathered crates lay on the jetties.

"Kind of strange," I whispered. "Everything looks untouched. But we know someone's down here. Why haven't they taken anything? Some of these things must be valuable."

"Certainly valuable for scientific research," Lilli said.

"Yes, also valuable for scientific research," I repeated, looking around in fascination. Suddenly, I faltered. Something had caught my attention. But I didn't really know what it was. Apparently, only my subconscious had noticed. Slowly, I spun in a circle and looked at everything again.

"Timmi?" asked Marvin. "Are you okay?"

Then I saw it.

 What had I noticed?

# Among the Guardians

Next to the door on the right side hung a small, rather inconspicuous box. But I had seen a box just like it recently in a completely different place: In the photo that showed the leader of the Guardians. It depicted him holding a small card in front of precisely such a device.

"This is a card reader," I said, walking up to it. "If you hold the right card in front of it, the door will open."

Suddenly, a light went on inside the house. A moment later, the card reader lit up green and the door began to open at almost the same time.

We pressed ourselves up against the wall next to the door, so that we would be hidden behind it as it swung open. It opened further and further until it finally touched the tips of my toes.

We heard voices. Someone rushed out of the house while the door began to close again.

In a moment, it would no longer hide us from view.

Please don't look at us, I thought.

I caught sight of the backs of two men in a strange uniform. They were briskly moving away from us, exchanging heated arguments, without looking back.

Quiet as a mouse, Lilli scurried to catch the door before it fell into the lock.

But the automated closing mechanism was too strong. Lilli moved onto the other side of the door, to shove against it with all her strength, but it just pushed her back - into the building!

Now Marvin and I also pulled on the door. But it did not budge an inch. It kept closing mercilessly.

*I have to jam something into the gap*, I thought. But it was already too late.

It was hard to stop myself from calling out Lilli's name. But the men would surely have heard us. The last thing I saw was Lilli's frightened face.

Then the door closed, its lock snapping shut.

Marvin looked desperate. Silently, I gave him a sign to follow me. I sneaked around the corner of the house and went a few steps farther, until I was sure we were out of earshot of the two men.

"Your walkie-talkie!" I whispered. Marvin dug it out of his belt pouch and handed it to me. "Lilli?" I spoke breathlessly into it.

"Yes, I'm here," she replied.

I was relieved. At least we could talk to her.

"Hide somewhere. I'm sure someone will come through the door soon enough, and then you can get out again."

❖ ❖ ❖

But Lilli wasn't really listening. In the room behind the door, she had found a flight of stairs leading down. It was clear that these stairs had been built long after the days of pirates. A cool light shone up from below. Lilli climbed down the steps and, for the second time that day, was absolutely astonished by what lay before her.

She found herself standing above an enormous hall.

To the left and right, stairs led further down, and directly in front of her, a walkway ran high across the space that lay below.

As if in a trance, she kept walking straight ahead. She couldn't take her eyes off the scene beneath her.

"What in the world is this place?" Lilli murmured.

❖ ❖ ❖

"Why doesn't she answer? Are the walls too thick?" I asked. Even to my own ears, I sounded desperate.

But Marvin didn't answer, either. He stared open-mouthed at something looming over us. I followed his gaze and could hardly believe my eyes.

"No way," I stammered.

❖ ❖ ❖

Lilli bent over the metal railing and looked at the room below her. At its center stood a huge globe with tiny lights flickering on and off. Curved walls served as huge shelves. They were packed with folders, some of which were marked with first and last names, while others only had a symbol. People in uniforms were bustling about everywhere.

"Do you know where we are?" she said into her walkie-talkie. "I think it's the Guardians' headquarters."

"Right," a deep voice suddenly said right next to her.

Lilli spun around and saw a man wearing one of those strange uniforms.

She backed away, stumbled, and landed hard on the metal grating.

But immediately she realized that she didn't need to be afraid of the man.

Why didn't Lilli need to fear him?

# The Plan

Lilli recognized the man's shoes.

"Ruo?" asked Lilli. "How did you get here?"

"After the Guardians captured me in the Bank of Pirates, I was taken here," he said, stepping out of the shadows. "Then they threw me into an old cell. But I managed to free myself and steal this uniform. That let me sneak around without being recognized right away."

"You really do look different," Lilli said.

"I should hope so. I cut my hair short, smeared black oil into it, and took off my sunglasses and my hat. But my rings won't come off."

"You need gloves," Lilli said, seeming distracted. She searched Ruo's face as though something wasn't right and she was trying to figure it out.

Then the walkie-talkie crackled, snapping Lilli out of her thoughts.

❖ ❖ ❖

"Lilli, you won't believe what we're seeing here," I said.

There was a ship, perched high above us on scaffolding. An old pirate ship, freshly restored. It even had new sails. Simply hoist them, and it would be ready to sail away. But that alone was not what blew me away. At the back of the ship, a name was unmistakably emblazoned above a large circular window that we knew only too well. It read: STAR RUNNER.

"We found the Star Runner. She's here. The Guardians fixed it up. She's like new," I called into the walkie-talkie.

"What?" crackled back at me.

"We're going aboard. We have to have a look!" I said.

❖ ❖ ❖

"Lotterlulu's old ship. She's here," Lilli told Ruo.

He seemed to know already. "Yes, Riverblood told me so after I was taken prisoner."

"Riverblood?" asked Lilli, completely perplexed.

Ruo bent down to Lilli, grabbed her shoulders and looked at her urgently.

"We don't have much time," he said. "Listen to me carefully. The Star Runner is seaworthy. This ship is our way out of here."

"An old pirate ship?"

"She's not just any ship."

"The four of us can't sail a pirate ship by ourselves," Lilli protested. "That's totally impossible."

"Not when it comes to the Star Runner. That ship was far ahead of its time. Even today, it still is the most advanced of its class ever built. After all, Lotterlulu had as much money as he needed to create a masterpiece."

"Stop it, this is ridiculous," whispered Lilli.

"Listen to me, this is what we'll do," he said. "You're right that this is the Guardians' headquarters. I have to destroy it, and I know how to. This entire island is volcanic in origin. The Guardians use the heat of the volcano to generate the power for this giant underground facility."

"But you don't want to hurt anyone."

"The volcano will only erupt in the cave," said Ruo. "Not on the island above. And as soon as I ... *optimize* ... the mixture of the supercritical water a little, an alarm will be triggered. There will be enough time to evacuate everyone."

"The supercritical *what*?"

Ruo straightened up again. "Come on, you have to get out of here now. We'll all meet up on the Star Runner."

"There's something else," Lilli said, pulling out the four metal pieces resembling a ninja star. "The trail of the documents leads to this symbol. Do you know it?"

Ruo's eyes widened. "Wait a minute," he said. "The star is made of four interlocking pieces. The segments that interlock look like hands. It reminds me of a painting called *The Four Captains*. You can see four hands on it, each grasping the arm of the next hand. For a long time, the painting hung in this very cave, until Lotterlulu bought it to give to Maria. Maybe there is a secret compartment in the frame of the painting, and this star is the key. That could be it, Lilli. The hiding place!"

"And where in the world can we find the painting?" asked Lilli.

"As I said, it once belonged to Maria and hung in her house, but they had to leave it behind when they fled."

"Then it could be anywhere by now."

"Right, but it is a clue," said Ruo. "One step after another. First, you have to get out of here." He showed Lilli a small plastic card. "This was in the uniform. It will open the door up above. Go, now!"

Lilli nodded, and they both ran. Back upstairs, Ruo walked toward the exit to hold the card in front of the reader.

"Stop!" said Lilli. "We have to hide."

Where did Ruo and Lilli hide (each in their own hiding place)?

**BONUS QUESTION** Which three things did Ruo and Lilli move (that have nothing to do with their hiding places?)

# In the Trap

While searching for hiding places, Lilli and Ruo moved a bottle on the small cabinet next to the grandfather clock, ripped a handle off the large cabinet (which wouldn't open), and bumped into one of the darts in the wall. Finally, Ruo hid in one of the barrels on the scale, which made it sink lower. Lilli dug into one of the sacks of cotton, making its fill level higher.

❖ ❖ ❖

Once we reached the deck of the Star Runner, Marvin and I walked the wooden planks in awe. The first and last time we had stood on this ship, it was walled in with stone. To hide the vessel, a church had been built around it. I knelt down and pressed my hand against the deck. Amazing, thinking of everything this ship must have experienced.

"Where is that wind coming from?" asked Marvin.

"From somewhere at the back of the cave. It blows toward the water, which means there must be a way out to the open sea. That's probably how the Star Runner got in here," I said.

"Yes, but this harbor hasn't been discovered in over a hundred years," Marvin mused. "The cave entrance must be camouflaged. But how?"

"No idea" I said. "But the ship is on a ramp, just waiting for someone to let it slide into the water and hoist the sails. Then I'm sure you could sail out of here. It wasn't restored just so someone could sail in circles around this cave."

My gaze fell to the helm.

A strange feeling spread through me. It had been a long time since I had held this steering wheel in my hands. Without taking my eyes off it, I slowly walked up the steps to the cabin deck. I saw the spokes that had been missing last time had been replaced, but the little numbers were still there.

I gripped the wheel as if I were the captain and let my gaze glide over the mighty deck in front of me. It was a moment I will never forget. Was I made for adventure? Of course I was!

"Timmi!" I heard Marvin call. He was standing at the main mast and gestured me to join him.

With a little sigh, I let go of the wheel. Then I ran to Marvin.

"Look, there are levers on these masts to set the sails," he said.

"Really? Normally, you'd need half the crew for that."

"If we can set sails and get the ship off the ramp, we might be able to sail it out of here," Marvin said, looking at me expectantly.

"What? No! Can I remind you how many of James Eckles' flying machines you destroyed last time? And now you want to steer a pirate ship?"

Marvin looked sadly at his feet. "If I hadn't flown the bumblebee, we couldn't have freed James Eckles," he said quietly.

"You're right. But a pirate ship is going a step too far. Anyway, come with me," I said encouragingly.

We ran down inside the ship and found the captain's cabin. As he had back then, Marvin stepped in front of the grand circular window and looked through it in amazement. The cabin had been faithfully restored to its original condition.

A great achievement, considering the ship had once been completely flooded - thanks to us blowing a hole in it.

"I wonder if they restocked the dynamite, too?" I asked with a grin.

"Here comes Lilli," said Marvin happily, still looking out the window. All of a sudden, his expression darkened.

"Watch out! Stop!"

❖ ❖ ❖

Lilli saw Marvin's silhouette behind the round bow window of the Star Runner and couldn't help smiling. Then, out of the corner of her eye, she noticed a movement to her left.

"Hello, Lilli!" said Shila. She was sitting on an electric motorcycle, which had let her approach silently. Uneasily, Lilli took a few steps back.

"The Guardians told me a lot about you. My name is..."

"Shila," said Lilli.

"How in the world did you know that?" she asked.

Instead of answering, Lilli looked Shila over with an assessing eye. She actually looked quite friendly. "Don't you have a bad conscience, working for people like that?" asked Lilli. "For the Guardians."

"I hate the Guardians," said Shila. "But sometimes, you have no choice."

"You're being forced?" asked Lilli. "Then help us!"

"Believe me, if I thought there was a real chance, I would," said Shila. "But there isn't any. Forget it."

Lilli sighed. "So, how did you find us?"

"I thought you were so clever," said Shila. "Do you know what my friends like about me? I'm good at listening."

At first, Lilli didn't understand. Then it dawned on her.

What helped Shila to find us?

# The Lion's Den

"Timmi's walkie-talkie. You found it in the Bank of Pirates," said Lilli. "Now it's in the pocket of your motorbike. You listened in on us."

"But not just that. After you used your walkie-talkies here in the cave, I was able to locate you based on signal strength and other parameters," Shila said. "Piece of cake."

As subtly as possible, Lilli looked past Shila to the bow window of the Star Runner.

❖ ❖ ❖

Marvin and I watched the scene below us, our hearts racing.

"Oh no, we have to help her!" I said.

"But how?" stammered Marvin.

I had no idea. But we had to do something. Marvin just looked at me with wide eyes, which upset me even more. "Let's go!" I yelled.

Marvin flinched away, frightened.

It didn't matter, I had to go to her. I spun around and ...

❖ ❖ ❖

My head was pounding. Slowly, I opened my eyes.

"Timmi!" said Lilli. "You're awake."

"Where am I? What happened?" I asked.

"You ran into a wall," said Marvin. "To be more specific, you hit your head on the wooden beam next to the bow window."

"How was *that* possible?" I asked, and gingerly felt my head. It had an impressive goose egg.

"No idea. But you sure did it," said Marvin.

"How's the head? Are you feeling sick?" asked Lilli.

Slowly, I sat up. Only now did I realize that I didn't know where we were. A hotel room? Lilli noticed my puzzled stare.

"Welcome to the Volante," Lilli said.

"To the what?" I asked.

"The ship of the Guardian Supreme," Lilli whispered.

I shuddered. My eyes jumped back and forth between Lilli and Marvin. Were they joking?

"Shila had the ship called because it has advanced medical equipment on board. Your head was scanned somehow. Looks like you're okay," Lilli said.

"The Guardians helped me?"

"They're not nice, though. We're prisoners here. They took the puzzle box away from us."

"And the head of the Guardians wants to see us," said Marvin. "As soon as you woke up."

Lilli bent down to me and whispered: "I don't know if they're listening to us. But Ruo is out there somewhere. He escaped and is looking for a way to destroy the cave. Because this is the Guardians' headquarters."

I looked at Lilli, startled. Um, *destroy*?

Then Marvin leaned over and whispered in my other ear, "But we still have the ninja star."

Quietly, Lilli told me everything she had experienced, seen and heard at the Guardians' headquarters.

A thousand questions shot through my mind. But before I could say anything, the door to our room swung open.

"Come with me," said a woman with a stern expression. She was wearing the uniform of the Guardians.

A few minutes later, we found ourselves in a large room located at the very bottom of the Volante. This had to be the private living quarters of the Guardian Supreme.

Parts of the floor and walls were made of thick glass panels. The sea behind was illuminated by floodlights, making it possible to see the fish that swam by. Old artifacts and paintings hung on the walls.

Awestruck, I tried to take in the room.

The woman who had escorted us in shut the door and left. We were about to meet the leader of the Guardians. The one person who had been pulling the strings in the background all these years, trying to derail our adventures over and over again.

Slowly, I went down the stairs.

"Wow," Marvin said excitedly. "Look at the fish! They're huge! Or does the glass make them look bigger?"

My attention was captured by something else, though.

"Um, Lilli," I said. "What did Ruo say to you again?"

"Why, when?" asked Lilli. "What's going on?"

 What was I alluding to?

# The Last Pirate

"The Four Captains," said Lilli, after I had pointed at the painting. "Four hands, each grasping the arm of the next hand. That must be it."

"Look how thick the frame is," I whispered.

"A secret compartment!" said Marvin. "Definitely a secret compartment."

Lilli examined the sides of the old frame and quickly found what she was looking for.

"Here," Lilli said. "A slot. That's where the star might fit."

Suddenly, we heard a series of beeps. A high-pitched tone, followed by a low-pitched tone, and twice a tone that was pitched somewhere between the first two.

The door next to us swung open and a man stepped through.

I estimated his age to be about thirty.

"This painting once belonged to Lotterlulu. Like so much in this room," he said, eyeing us. "I took it. Just as I took the casket from you."

Lilli crossed her arms and asked angrily, "And where is our casket now?"

"I have... repurposed it," he said with a smirk.

I took a deep breath and asked, "Who are you?"

"Many call me the Guardian Supreme."

"You can't be," Lilli said. "Ruo showed us a photo of the Guardian Supreme. An old man. With black eyes and a black mouth."

"Ruo, hmm? That's what he calls himself. Ruo Tultell, right?"

"You should know. After all, you're the one holding him captive," I replied.

"Well, as you know, he has already freed himself and is presently trying to escape."

He *knew* that? I tried to keep a straight face.

"Ruo Tultell," repeated the leader of the Guardians, and picked up a piece of chalk. He wrote the name on a chalkboard and looked at it for a while.

"Funny," he finally said, and smiled. Then he turned back to us. "You three have caused me and my organization a lot of headaches. You found the book. El Iksir. You freed James Eckles and put Dr. Sangrey behind bars. And you set police all over the world on me. And why? Do you know what El Iksir actually contains?"

"A collection of elixirs," I said, repeating what Ruo had told us.

"The formulas can only be read by someone who can correctly decode the writing," said the Guardian Supreme, and nodded.

"Is it true?" I asked. "That one of them brings eternal life?"

"Correct. Elixir number one. The Elixir of Eternity. Eternal life. But what is life without youth? You get older and older, your skin wrinkles and hangs loose. When you're past 150, your eyes and mouth eventually turn black."

"You're kidding," Lilli whispered. "More than 150?"

"It sounds better than it feels, believe me."

"How...how old are you?" Marvin asked hesitantly.

"Don't be fooled," Lilli hissed.

"This first elixir formed the foundation of the Guardians' power. Virtually every influential person wanted to prolong their life, so they depended on our favor.

"But elixirs two and three remained unattainable. That only changed with the brilliant James Eckles, who finally decoded the second elixir, the *Elixir of Knowledge*. It unlocks the potential of the human mind. If you took it, you could suddenly understand everything, learn everything, as though your mental potential had been expanded exponentially. Even the most complex maze of logic becomes straightforward. You could master mathematics, physics within a few days. But you already know that, don't you?"

I nodded silently. This elixir really existed. In our last adventure, we had freed James Eckles from the Guardians' clutches, and he had told us about the elixir. We didn't have any reason to doubt him.

"Unfortunately, anyone who consumes the elixir loses most of their memories after a few weeks. One of my subordinates, poor Dr. Sangrey, now thinks he's living in the eighteenth century. But my scientists, who have taken the Elixir of Knowledge and unleashed their cognitive abilities, finally managed to wrest the secret of the third elixir from the book: the *Elixir of Youth*."

"It lets old people become young again?" I asked.

"The black eyes disappear, the black mouth, the wrinkles, the gray hair. It takes two days, and then you're like new again," said the Guardian Supreme. His eyes sparkled with excitement. "It starts from the inside. Like a light that grows in the center of the body and then begins to radiate outward. The muscles, the tendons, the bones and all the internal organs grow strong and healthy again. Then the change can be seen from the outside as well. It happens very quickly. The skin becomes taut and the hair regains its old color."

Grinning, he continued, "Hah! The hair! At the end of the rejuvenation, it sprouts like a weed. It's incredible, you can watch it grow. A couple of inches in just a few minutes."

Suddenly, the Guardian Supreme clapped his hands firmly together, making me flinch.

"Then it's complete!" he said. "You are renewed."

"And have to get a haircut," Lilli said. "What nonsense."

The Guardian Supreme shrugged. "Believe what you want. But basically, modern science is on the trail of these mysteries today, too. Ever heard of Yamanaka factors?"

Lilli pressed her lips together. She probably hadn't.

"So you took this elixir? That's why you're young again?" she asked.

"I am the leader of the Guardians and the last true pirate."

"You are..." I said, not daring to continue.

"Riverblood," Marvin stammered, his eyes wide.

"Riverblood," he confirmed with a smile.

"This is all nonsense," Lilli hissed, crossing her arms. "If you're Riverblood - how did Lotterlulu know you and your pirates were coming to get Maria that night? What tipped him off?"

"You are well informed. On that night, I also took the painting you are standing in front of. I took it from the house Maria was hiding in. As well as the answer to your question, which you can see hanging back there," Riverblood said, pointing.

Only now did we notice the little bell that hung framed above the door. Our eyes all widened in astonishment.

It had to be the alarm bell whose thread Riverblood had cut all those years ago.

Suddenly, the light around us turned reddish and an announcement rang out, "Red alert. Everyone to their posts."

"Excuse me, I'll be right back," Riverblood said, hurrying up the stairs and through the top door.

"What's going on?" I asked.

"Ruo," Lilli and Marvin answered at the same time.

For a brief moment, no one spoke a word. We just stood there, trying to think clearly.

"We have to hurry," Lilli finally said, turning back to the painting. "No matter what, we need these documents."

She took the metal star out of her pocket. With trembling fingers, she tried to insert it into the slot hidden in the frame.

"It fits," she said, pushing the star in as far as it would go. It made a *click*.

"What was that?" asked Marvin. "The springs on the side didn't move. Maybe the mechanism is jammed."

Marvin felt along the underside of the frame.

"There's something here," he said, pulling on it.

A hidden part of the frame slid out. In front of us lay a collection of wooden keys with letters on them. There was also a metal plaque. On it was written:

*We throw it away when we need it.*
*We take it back when we are done with it.*

"A riddle," I said. "We have to press the keys to write the word that will solve it."

"Uhm, what was the name of the painting again?" asked Marvin.

What word was the solution?

# Code Red

"The painting is called The Four Captains," I said. "So the puzzle might have something to do with seafaring. I think the solution could be "*anchor*." You let it go when you need it."

"And haul it back in when you're done with it," Marvin said.

I excitedly pressed the buttons, only to hesitate before the last letter. *Hopefully the solution is correct*, I thought. Then I took a deep breath and pressed the key.

Immediately, the upper edge of the frame folded apart. Inside lay something. A kind of glass flask with a cork stopper. Not even a second later, the springs on the sides released and catapulted the ancient bottle high into the air.

"Whoa!" I exclaimed, reaching out my arm to catch it. It spun around a few times and then landed right between my fingers. Excitedly, we looked at our find.

"What's in it?" asked Marvin.

"Paper," said Lilli. "A thick roll of paper. This must be it."

"Yes!" I said. "The secret documents that can take down the Guardians!"

"And Riverblood had them hanging in his own living room the entire time," Marvin said, his eyes wide.

"Now let's get out of here," Lilli said. "Ruo wanted to meet up with us on the Star Runner."

When we arrived at the upper door, Lilli slowly pushed the handle down and opened it just a crack. Behind it lay a long hallway. Rooms opened off of it to the right and left, and at the end was a large staircase. People were scurrying hectically back and forth.

"We have to get to the steps," Lilli whispered. "They lead all the way up. That's the way out."

"But we'll never make it," Marvin said. "There are people everywhere. They'll catch us."

"I don't think so," Lilli mused. "They're all busy with more important things right now."

Suddenly, a loud drone sounded from the ship's loudspeakers:

*Evacuation of headquarters initiated. All aboard the Volante. Repeat: All aboard the Volante.*

"Maybe we'd better stay here, too," whispered Marvin. "Who knows what's going on out in the cave."

"And what will happen to us and the documents then? We just have to get to the Star Runner," said Lilli. "Ruo was sure he could sail us out of the cave."

"Let's try," I said. "We'll just walk through and pretend nothing is wrong. Like we're allowed to walk around here."

Marvin hesitated, but he finally nodded. Lilli started walking quickly, and Marvin and I stayed directly behind her. We headed down the narrow corridor further and further toward the staircase.

*WHAM!*

A dull thud was followed by a deep rumble, making the ship tremble. *What was that?* People clung to the walls and looked around uncertainly.

"Run!" I shouted and we sprinted as fast as we could. Surely no one would pay attention to us now.

The staircase seemed endless. It led higher and higher from level to level. Finally, we reached the upper deck.

What we saw then made our blood run cold.

The walls of the cave, which had been shrouded in darkness before, were now bathed in a fiery red light. A glowing substance was swelling out of the rock. In some places, it was even flowing out of the cave roof. Some of the houses built into the steep slopes were surrounded by the stream. They were breaking apart and crashing down in a stony avalanche.

"Lava," whispered Lilli.

There was another deep rumble, then a loud, dull bang, and we saw glowing shards fly through the air. From all around the cave, the Guardians' henchmen hurried toward the Volante and hastily scrambled aboard over a wide plank.

"Come on!" I shouted. "To the Star Runner!"

"But how do we know Ruo made it on board?" Marvin yelled, holding my arm tightly.

I glanced at the ship. The Star Runner stood unchanged on its ramp, seemingly just waiting to sail us out of this mess.

But Marvin was right. Without Ruo, it wouldn't work. Then Lilli noticed something.

"Someone has definitely been on the Star Runner after us," Lilli asserted. "I can see three things that prove it."

What three things did Lilli mean?

 Find one           Find two          Find all three

# A Narrow Escape

"That one window was closed before, the ladder is gone from the center mast, and the anchor isn't in the water now," said Lilli, as we walked briskly to the ramp.

Numerous henchmen of the Guardians poured aboard the Volante, while we squeezed past them in the opposite direction. When we finally arrived below, we ran as fast as we could.

Halfway there, I noticed a shadow flitting across the roofs of the harbor buildings. And in the next moment, Shila leaped down in front of our feet.

"Wrong way!" she said.

"Let us through," I demanded.

"You must not board the Star Runner," she said.

"You seriously want to deliver us to Riverblood?" Lilli yelled.

"He's going to destroy the Star Runner. That was his plan from the beginning," Shila said "He's been talking about it for weeks, calling it his Project *Grand Slam*. The fact that Ruo escaped from his cell is also part of it. You must not go on that ship."

"You're lying," I shouted.

"Riverblood has an old score to settle with this Ruo. He wants him to escape on the Star Runner – just so he can sink the ship right after he does," Shila said.

Another explosion rocked the ground beneath us.

"Riverblood certainly didn't plan the destruction of his headquarters," Lilli exclaimed. "And we have the documents that can bring him down. We need to get them to safety."

Shila's eyes widened.

"What?" she asked, "How could you possibly find them?"

"We're good at finding things," Marvin exclaimed.

This information seemed to change everything for Shila. She stared at us in shock. For a few seconds, she fell silent, clearly thinking hard. Then she reached a decision: "Get on the Star Runner. I'll try to help you from here. If you have these documents, we might really have a chance to defeat the Guardians."

"Let's go!" I shouted, and we ran past Shila.

"Hurry!" Ruo called as he watched us rush up the stairs to the Star Runner. "We have to get out of here, and fast." He stood behind the wheel and held some kind of remote control. We were barely on board when he yelled, "Get below deck. Run down and hold on to something."

We stumbled down the steps into the ship. At that moment, we heard a dull thud. But this time, it didn't sound like it came from somewhere far away in the cave. It seemed very close. Ruo must have initiated the launch with his remote control.

The ship tilted forward with such a violent jerk that we all lost our balance and fell to the floor. We immediately grabbed at the old wooden floorboards, jamming our fingers into the cracks, trying to find a grip.

Now the Star Runner picked up speed and thundered down the ramp. The noise around us became deafening.

We screamed like banshees as the top of the ship first dug deep into the water, then immediately popped back up. All the furniture that was not fastened down was thrown around wildly. Rumbling and crashing sounds came from all around us.

But just as quickly, everything was quiet again. When we stepped back onto the upper deck, Ruo had already hoisted all the sails. I marveled at the ingenious system of pulleys on board the Star Runner. A single person could ready the ship, working all alone.

Wind had caught the large sails, and we were heading at a considerable speed toward the cave entrance, which was only open a crack. It was a massive gate, its metal substructure coated with stone from the outside, making it indistinguishable from the surrounding real cliffs - a perfect camouflage. But I looked anxiously at the gate, because it wasn't opening any further. There was no way we could fit through as it was.

"This doesn't look good," I murmured. "Not good at all."

❖ ❖ ❖

Shila stood in the control room of the cave gate, located in the building next to it. The quake from the last explosion had produced a short circuit, causing the gate to stop opening. The Guardians had sent her for one simple reason: Since she had a motorcycle, she could move through the cave faster than anyone else. Now she was in radio contact with the technician in charge on the Volante. She already knew which backup unit she had to activate to get the gate working again. But she didn't like what she saw.

"You're kidding me," she said into her radio.

"I'm completely serious. The red module has to go into the slot at the right. To do this, you need to move the other modules out of the way. But you can only slide each of them in the direction of the arrows. Think hard! Find a way!"

 Which blue modules must be moved, and how, for the red module to be slid all the way to the right?

# Not Quite Fair

She slid the red module a little to the right, so that she could pull down module number 01. This created the space to move module 02 to the left into the corner. Now she could push module 06 all the way up, freeing up space to slide module 09 to the left. Next, she moved module 07 up and module 08 down. This cleared the way for the red module. She slid it into the slot at the right, and the massive machinery ground back into motion.

❖ ❖ ❖

"The gate is opening again," I yelled to Ruo, who was standing above at the helm.

"That was a close one," he answered. At that moment, the gate revealed the open sea, and the warm rays of the evening sun hit our faces. Ruo yelled for sheer joy, and I cheered with him. We had done it. Marvin clapped his hands and bobbed up and down, blinking at the bright sunlight. Lilli grinned with relief.

As the Star Runner passed the gate, I noticed a green motorcycle zooming at breakneck speed along a road built into the cliffs of the cave, racing back toward the harbor. It was Shila! Was she heading for the Volante? *Hopefully she makes it out of the cave*, I thought.

"Hey," Lilli whispered, suddenly standing next to me along with Marvin. "There is something else I've been meaning to tell you. We're not out of the woods yet."

"Why? We just need to get the documents to safety," I said. "Then we've won."

"It's about Ruo," Lilli said. "Look at him."

I turned and eyed him closely.

"Don't you think he's changed somehow?" Lilli asked.

"Of course he has. He cut his hair in his cell and shaved his beard. He told you himself. He isn't wearing his hat anymore and his sunglasses are gone," I whispered, and shrugged. "Of course he looks different."

"But the short hair, and the stubble," said Lilli.

"Are black," Marvin said, completing Lilli's sentence.

My gaze traveled back to Ruo. Then he glanced at me, too.

"Timmi," Ruo called. "Come over here for a moment."

"I'm going to take a closer look," I whispered, and started going over. Lilli and Marvin followed along.

When I stood face to face with Ruo, I was surprised at how different he now looked. His hair was as black as coal.

"Timmi, you still have the necklace I gave you, don't you?" he asked me urgently.

"Of course," I said, fishing it out from under my shirt.

"Please give it back to me," he said.

I pulled the necklace up over my head and handed it to him. He briefly examined the pendant and then hung it around his neck.

"Thank you, Timmi," he said. "This is really important."

"What's that all about?" I asked. "With the necklace."

Ruo gave me a furtive look. He seemed to be considering whether he could trust us with its meaning.

"The liquid in the pendant," I said. "Is that one of the elixirs? Did you take some of the elixirs, too?"

"What?" said Ruo. "What makes you think that?"

"Your hair. It's black. The Elixir of Youth can do things like–" I said.

"My hair? That's some nasty old black oil," Ruo said. "Lubricating oil. So I won't be recognized. Touch it!"

At the same moment, a heavy detonation roared from behind us. We spun around and ducked. Fire spewed out of the cave gate, where we had sailed out mere minutes ago. We were struck by a hot, stinking blast wave, and small pieces of broken rock splashed into the water all around us. Thick, gray smoke rose from the gate.

"What on earth have you done?" hissed Lilli.

"I didn't plan for it to be like that," Ruo said with concern. "I hope they all made it."

"They did, old friend," a tinny voice sounded overhead. We squinted into the sun and spotted a loudspeaker on the first mast.

"Riverblood," Ruo muttered.

Suddenly, something surfaced out of the sea about a thousand feet in front of the Star Runner. It was the Volante and it rose higher and higher out of the water. Only now did I realize how much larger than the Star Runner it was. Like a mighty gray rock, it now lay calmly in the water while we cruised ever closer to it, driven by the wind in our sails.

"Look in the compartment behind the wheel," said Riverblood.

Ruo looked extremely tense. He took a deep breath, reached into the little compartment, and discovered a radio. He pressed his lips together and hesitated briefly. Then he pushed the button to speak: "Well, did your cave get a bit too hot and bright for you, Riverblood?"

"Of course not. Don't you remember I took your sunglasses? One of the lenses broke, but they suit me. I'll keep them as a souvenir. And today is a wonderful day. A long-cherished wish will be fulfilled. The good old Star Runner, Lotterlulu's pride and joy, will be blasted to the waterline by my cannons. With you on board. A dream come true."

Ruo gave us a dark look. "I have some cannons here too, you know," he finally said.

"Right. I had them all restored. The whole ship is in pristine condition," Riverblood said. "You even have gunpowder. Everything you need for your last stand, old friend. A fair fight. Almost fair, at least."

Ruo pulled me close to him. "You'll steer the ship, do you hear me?" he said, turning the wheel a little, until finally we were heading straight for the Volante. "Sail straight ahead. Whatever you do, don't swerve!"

*Excuse me?*

He gave me a pat on the back.

"Marvin, Lilli, you're coming with me," he said and sprinted off with my friends in tow.

"Are you trying to ram me?" the loudspeaker crackled.

I gulped. Was I really supposed to talk to the Guardian Supreme? I took a deep breath, closed my eyes and exhaled slowly. It didn't help much. "Um, hello," I said.

"Who is that?" asked Riverblood.

"Um, it's me, Timmi," I said, my voice trembling.

"He let you take the helm?"

"Looks like it. Not a good idea, right?"

"Interesting. Then he'll go to the cannons. He won't like what he's about to find there. And you should turn that wheel."

❖ ❖ ❖

Ruo, Lilli, and Marvin hurried to the second lower deck. "Pay attention," Ruo called. "Riverblood will prepare to dive soon. He will want to destroy the Star Runner with cannons, not have it sink in a collision."

"Are you sure?" asked Marvin.

"Well, pretty sure. It would be like him. He's always been a show-off," Ruo said. "A firefight with the Volante is practically hopeless. I was able to obtain the Volante's construction plans some time ago, and I have studied them thoroughly. The only vulnerable spot is the rear propulsion system – the turbines. But that's our chance. When the Volante resurfaces, they will lie directly in front of our rear cannons. We'll have to load them, but there's not much time left to -"

At that moment, Ruo's gaze fell on a closed metal gate with a keypad.

"You've got to be kidding me," he said. "The cannons are right behind those bars. He's blocked our access."

"Probably to prevent you from doing exactly what you were going to do," said Lilli. "He'll only open this door when he has you right where he wants you."

Ruo quickly pressed a few random buttons on the keypad, each emitting a differently pitched beep, and then pressed the green button. The display lit up red, indicating an incorrect code had been entered - and that four digits were required.

"I guess we're done for," Ruo stammered.

"Wait, we heard beeps like that today before," said Marvin. He pushed buttons one, five, and nine. One made the highest beep, and nine the lowest. "If we're lucky, I have an idea what the code is."

 What was the access code?

# The Last Battle

"Riverblood's lucky numbers! Two, six, and nine. That's how he chose the date to kidnap Maria. And when we were on the Volante earlier, we heard Riverblood use his personal code. It was a higher beep, a really low beep, and then two beeps that sounded the same and were somewhere in the middle," explained Marvin. "If Riverblood's code is his lucky numbers, it must be two, nine, six, six."

As he spoke, Marvin had already entered the numbers. He pressed the button to confirm the code. Immediately, the display lit up green and the door unlocked.

"Bingo!" said Marvin, grinning.

"Sometimes you really do come in handy," said Lilli with an appreciative smile.

"Let's go!" Ruo yelled, yanking open the door.

❖ ❖ ❖

"Turn!" the loudspeaker above me crackled.

"No!" I repeated.

"The Star Runner will crash into my ship and break into a thousand pieces. Turn aside!"

Riverblood was surely right. The Volante seemed like an indestructible monstrosity, and I was steering an old wooden ship directly at it. At high speed.

"I'd rather not," I answered, and gulped. Where was Ruo? We were about to collide!

"You've got to be kidding me!" Riverblood screamed.

"Unbelievable, isn't it?" I said, and I really meant it. If something didn't happen soon, I would simply have to turn the Star Runner away, trying to evade the collision. Was that even still possible? No more than ten seconds remained before we would crash.

"Dive!" yelled Riverblood.

*Yes!* I thought. *And it had better be quick!*

To my relief, the humungous Volante sank fast. Only a few seconds later, it was completely submerged and the Star Runner was plowing through the sea right above it. But then I heard a scraping sound, coming from far below me. The Volante wasn't deep enough yet! Everything vibrated, and the Star Runner suddenly shot seven feet up into the air and at the same time it tilted to the side. Startled, I clung to the steering wheel.

This couldn't end well.

But it did. Shortly afterward, the ship sank back down, swayed back and forth a little, then sailed on as though nothing had happened.

❖ ❖ ❖

"Watch out, he's surfacing again," Ruo called out. "Stand by!"

From the rear cannon ports, Lilli, Marvin and Ruo watched as the Volante rose out of the sea.

Now they had a clear shot at its turbines.

"Fire!" shouted Ruo.

Nervous but determined, Lilli held a burning torch, eying the fuses of the five rear cannons. She walked across the room without stopping, touching the torch against each of the fuses. All five burned quickly toward the cannons.

"Cover your ears!" Ruo yelled.

❖ ❖ ❖

I flinched. The Star Runner was shaking. At the same time, I heard a series of explosions. Had the Volante fired at us? She had surfaced again.

Then, just for a moment, for the blink of an eye, I could make out the heavy black cannonballs flying straight toward the Volante with impossible speed. The impact was instantaneous. The Volante's turbines seemed to explode from within, torn into pieces that flew high up in the air.

Instinctively, I ducked, but the chunks splashed into the water at a safe distance. Then everything was silent.

The Volante lay motionless. We had won! The old Star Runner had actually done it!

From somewhere below me, I heard Lilli, Marvin and Ruo whooping and hollering. I joined in, cheering as loud as I could.

Shortly after, the three of them came back on deck. I hugged my friends while Ruo, smiling with satisfaction, pulled some levers to haul in the sails. He didn't want to leave the Volante just yet. Not without taking a little time to enjoy his victory. He leaned against the railing and watched the Volante bobbing along in the sunset.

"A wonderful last battle," Ruo murmured. Suddenly, his face darkened. "Who in the world is *that*?" he asked, looking nervously toward the island.

I could hear them before I saw them. Three helicopters in flight. Three matte black, unmarked helicopters.

"The Guardians?" I asked. "A rescue squad for Riverblood?"

"No idea," said Ruo.

"Maybe we should hoist the sails again," said Marvin.

"No, we certainly couldn't escape them," Ruo whispered.

Two of the helicopters eventually positioned themselves over the Volante and one hovered close beside the Star Runner.

With a jerk, the side door of the helicopter opened. I immediately recognized the uniforms worn by the special forces team.

"UNITE!" I shouted. "They're on our side!"

In the middle of the opening stood a woman with blond hair.

"That's Commissioner Hallewell!" exclaimed Lilli, laughing and waving at her.

"Sir London reached them!" Marvin said, bobbing and clapping. "But they could have come a little sooner."

The helicopter rose up so that it was hovering above us and let down a rope. Commissioner Hallewell and two other members of UNITE slid down it.

"Hello everyone," Commissioner Hallewell called out, "Are you all right? Everyone unharmed?"

We nodded happily.

"How did you get here so fast?" I asked.

"Oh, our team has been on the island for quite some time. We suspected the Guardians' headquarters must be around here somewhere."

"But the headquarters are gone," said Marvin.

"I'm sure it won't matter. The Volante should give us enough evidence to smash the organization once and for all."

"Unless the evidence is being destroyed right now," Ruo said.

"As you can see, we are hurrying to prevent this," she said, jerking her head toward the Volante.

I could see scores of special forces personnel rappelling down from the other two helicopters.

"This should help, too," I said, showing her the ancient bottle containing the documents.

"What's that supposed to be?"

"It's a list of everyone from the first years of the organization, and of all their bank accounts," said Ruo. "Many of the banks still exist today. That will help you to bring light into the darkness."

"The money trail," said Commissioner Hallewell. Grabbing her ear she said: "Understood. I'm coming over."

Then she turned back to us. "The crew is cooperating. It seems the big boss has locked himself in his room, which is secured with an access code."

"If we tell you the code, can we come with you?" asked Marvin.

She laughed and said, "Agreed."

"I'll stay here and take care of the ship," Ruo said.

"Can you steer it into the island's harbor, then?" Commissioner Hallewell asked.

"But of course," Ruo replied. "No problem."

He took a deep breath. His eyes jumped back and forth between Lilli, Marvin and me.

"It was truly a pleasure, getting to know you all," he said.

"Timmi, you are extraordinary. But remember to always believe in yourself. The next time you're afraid, don't forget that this feeling can be helpful. Listen to yourself and ask yourself what's worrying you. Keep looking deeper until you've found and, most importantly, understood the reason. Then the knot in your stomach will often come undone all by itself," Ruo said. "Of course, I'm not talking about the moments when a volcano is exploding all around you."

To be honest, I wasn't entirely sure what Ruo was trying to say to me. But there would come a time when I would think back on his words, and I could always draw courage from them.

"Marvin," said Ruo, and smiled. "You can be pretty sassy. But most of all, you have a big heart. You're a really good friend. The kind of friend everyone wishes they had. Stay the way you are, and you'll never be alone. And believe me, that's important."

Then Ruo turned to Lilli. At that moment, I didn't understand what was going on with him. But he simply looked at her and pressed his lips together. Then he took a step toward her and hugged her tightly. I think his eyes were wet. He smiled at Lilli and nodded to her. She returned his nod, as if the two of them had come to an understanding without saying a word.

"It's not as though we'll never see each other again," Lilli said. But somehow it sounded more like a question.

"You have to go now," said Ruo, handing us over to the care of Commissioner Hallewell.

❖ ❖ ❖

After being pulled one by one into the helicopter above us (via a vest secured to a pulley system), it wasn't long before we were facing Riverblood in his study on the Volante. It was a bright room that contained all sorts of artifacts. Commissioner Hallewell had already confronted Riverblood with various accusations and now came to her last point.

"Last but not least we know about the red-haired young woman in green leather gear, who rides an electric motorcycle. She handled the grunt work for you today."

*Where in the world is Shila?* I wondered.

Riverblood took a deep breath, and his eyes flickered threateningly over the three of us kids.

Then he began: "This is all ridiculous. First, I didn't do anything to this Ruo. I didn't lie to him, didn't threaten him, didn't insult him, didn't take anything from him, and I certainly didn't imprison him. Never even met him in person.

"Second, I don't know any Shila either. I have many employees, but a young motorcyclist in green leather, with red hair at that, would certainly have stuck in my mind.

"Third, I extensively restored the Star Runner. That cost a fortune. I never planned to shoot and sink it. What rubbish.

"Fourth, there were no illegal activities at our research station. No extortion, no bribery - nothing like that. My organization harvested energy from the heat of the volcano. Carbon-neutral. With this technology, we can alleviate the problems of mankind. At least we could have, because now, unfortunately, our facility has been destroyed.

"And fifth, I don't know anything about a Bank of Pirates, let alone a puzzle box or these ominous documents that everything is supposed to lead to."

**How many of Riverblood's statements can you disprove or cast doubt on, and why?**

One     Two or three     Four     All five (almost impossible)

# Settling the Score

*He's lying, and I can prove it,* I thought. *Just you wait!*

I took a deep breath and was about to list the evidence when Riverblood looked at me. Although his face seemed relaxed, there was a dark rage in his eyes. It hit me at full force. The words stayed stuck in my throat. I grabbed my inhaler and took a deep drag.

"It's strange, isn't it?" he said. "That this Shila is nowhere to be found. I hope nothing has happened to her."

I gulped. That was a warning!

"How dare you?" said Commissioner Hallewell. "Don't try to intimidate the children. I won't let you get away with that."

But it was too late. Lilli and I looked at each other. *Where was Shila?*

"You see," Riverblood said, addressing Commissioner Hallewell. "It's like this: The volcanic explosion pulverized everything in the cave. Even if there had been some sort of evidence there, it's been destroyed now. You understand?"

"You're forgetting my witnesses," Commissioner Hallewell said.

"Your so-called witnesses, the three children and some fellow called Ruo, apparently broke into my research facility and caused a volcanic eruption that has set research into green energy sources back by years. It's only thanks to luck that no one was hurt. And you're basing your charges on *these* witnesses?"

Commissioner Hallewell looked over at us. She looked unsettled. "Aren't you going to say something?" she asked, "Did you notice anything about his statements?"

I wanted to speak, but I was afraid. I'm sure Lilli and Marvin were too.

*Don't chicken out now*, I thought. What had Ruo said? You should face your fears. I closed my eyes and tried to concentrate.

"And, Commissioner," Riverblood continued. "It appears you are also illegally occupying my ship. Do you have a search warrant?"

*Could we kids really help convict the leader of one of the most powerful shadow organizations in the world? And what about Shila?* The more I thought about it, the more I understood why I was so afraid. But at the same time, I felt calmer. But why? It seemed completely illogical to me.

"I don't have a warrant. As the head of UNITE, I don't need one," Commissioner Hallewell said.

"Oh, but that's not quite true," Riverblood said. "You may only intervene without a warrant if there is a probable cause to believe that a person is in danger or that valuable evidence is about to be destroyed. But I see no justification here. Even your would-be witnesses are silent."

"I see plenty of justification," said Commissioner Hallewell.

"None that would hold up in any court, and you know it," said Riverblood.

I was still standing there, eyes closed, trying to find my courage. But would it put Shila in danger if I spoke up? In the end, she had helped us.

"Now leave my ship," said Riverblood. "That little one is about to fall over."

Then I felt Lilli take my hand and lightly squeeze it.

"Timmi?" asked Marvin. He put his arm around my shoulder. "Don't worry. We can just leave. Everything will be okay."

Without opening my eyes, I took a deep breath in. I breathed out. The fear was still there. But somehow, it was different. Smaller. It felt okay to be afraid.

"So, first of all," I said, my eyes still closed. "I can't prove that you met Ruo in person today."

"Right, little man," whispered Riverblood. "Behave yourself. And now, out with you, all of you."

Lilly squeezed my hand hard. She knew what was about to happen.

"But it is strange that his sunglasses are hanging on your collar," I said, and opened my eyes, still looking down at the ground. "And I bet that Ruo's fingerprints are on them, which would prove that they're his. Did he give them to you willingly? Or did you steal them from him?"

"You little weasel, I found those and -" Riverblood said, but was interrupted by Commissioner Hallewell.

"Now it's Timmi's turn!" she said.

"Secondly, you know the red-haired motorcyclist very well," I continued. "Or would you like to explain how you know her name? Commissioner Hallewell hadn't mentioned it."

"That's true!" she said in surprise.

"Of course you mentioned her name," said Riverblood.

"No, I didn't," she said.

I was still looking down at the floor. That helped.

"Third," I said, "it was Shila who told us about your plan to sink the Star Runner. The plan even had a name: *Grand Slam*."

"Never heard of it," hissed Riverblood. Now his rage was clear even in his voice.

Without looking up, I said: "But it's written in big, bright letters on one of the monitors above your desk. You can see the reflection in the windowpane."

"Indeed!" exclaimed Commissioner Hallewell. "Then there will certainly be more about this plan on your computer."

"Fourth," Lilli said.

It made me smile that she was brave enough to speak now too, and I squeezed her hand firmly to support her.

"Fourth, I bet there were illegal activities in your headquarters. On a big screen, there was something about an *Operation Tornado*. It also said the president of the island was going to be bribed. We saw posters of him everywhere. What was his name?"

"Ingvar," I said.

"Right, President Ingvar," said Lilli.

"The cave is destroyed," Riverblood growled. "Along with everything in it."

"There, sure, everything is destroyed. But not here. On the big screen in the cave, I saw the symbol of a tornado. I can see the same symbol on the file folder on your desk. I bet it contains everything about your bribery plan."

Riverblood snorted contemptuously.

"Fifth," said Marvin with a steady voice, as though he was now finally ready to say something too. "Fifth, you do know about the puzzle box. You took it from us and repurposed it. That's what you called it. Repurposed. Bad luck for you that I like animals so much. You have a nice aquarium. It has our box in it. You probably threw it in there as a decoration."

"The puzzle box is in the aquarium?" Commissioner Hallewell asked.

"Yup," said Marvin, sounding almost cheerful.

"And finally," I said, and raised my head to look Riverblood right in the eyes. His rage no longer had any power over me. I would win this duel, no doubt. "If you really don't know what the puzzle box led to: It's these documents right here!"

Then I raised up the ancient bottle that I still held in my hand and turned it over between my fingers.

Suddenly, Riverblood turned pale. He continued to lean against his desk, but somehow seemed to slump. With one arm, he propped himself up on the tabletop.

"The little one is about to fall over," Lilli said, and eyed Riverblood with contempt.

"Riverblood," said Commissioner Hallewell, "What did you say so aptly before? I may intervene if there is a probable cause to believe that valuable evidence is about to be destroyed. Well, I think the cause has been shown to be sufficiently probable."

Commissioner Hallewell made a hand gesture to the UNITE forces, who had positioned themselves at the door of the room.

In disbelief, Riverblood watched two of them spring into action, plainly with the intent of taking him into custody.

"And now" said Commissioner Hallewell, "you are under arrest."

Riverblood shook his head as though it was all a bad joke. "I know all the important politicians, everyone who matters in business. They all dance to my tune."

"I'm sure they'll be glad to be rid of you," Commissioner Hallewell said.

Handcuffs clicked on Riverblood's wrists.

"No, no, no," Riverblood said. "You can't do that. Not to me!"

"And all this because your organization tried to drive my grandpa out of his house," Lilli said.

"I don't have a clue who your grandpa is. I don't concern myself with trivialities," Riverblood scoffed.

I gasped. Could it be?

"Does that mean you don't know who Lilli is? What family she comes from?" I asked.

"Who is she supposed to be? I know all the important families. She's a nobody!" Riverblood screamed.

"She's a Lotterlulu," said Marvin. At that, he smiled, clapped his hands softly and bobbed up and down.

Riverblood stared at us, his eyes wide. "That can't be true," he finally said.

"Why else would the Bank of Pirates help us? Only Lotterlulu himself or one of his descendants could be given the second part of the treasure map," I said.

"Exactly," said Riverblood, to my surprise.

Lilli had already dug the report proving her relationship to Lotterlulu out of her backpack and now held it wordlessly under his nose.

"This settles it," she said, allowing Riverblood to study the document for a moment.

Then he turned as white as chalk.

"Destiny," murmured Riverblood. "A circle of fate hundreds of years in the making. Fascinating."

Suddenly, he froze.

"But that means Maria was expecting a child when I..." stuttered Riverblood. "*That's* why Lotterlulu threw it all away and didn't want to be a pirate anymore."

"It was a bad idea, messing with the Lotterlulu family," Lilli said. "Back then, and now, too."

"After Lotterlulu disappeared, I was the last great pirate," Riverblood said. "Nothing and no one could stop me."

"Until today," Lilli hissed.

"This is not the end," said Riverblood. He bent down to Lilli and whispered: "You always meet twice in life."

"We've already met twice today," said Lilli. "So that's done. Just like you and your Guardians."

"Take him away!" Commissioner Hallewell said.

Two members of the special forces grabbed Riverblood by the shoulders and briskly pushed him past us.

"I'm not gone forever, little Lotterlulu," Riverblood screamed. "I'll be back! Everything that he can do, I can do!"

Then he was led out of the room. For a few moments, we could still hear him raging and then, finally, it became quiet.

"I just hope that's the end of the Guardians," I said.

"You can count on that. We've seen the last of them," Commissioner Hallewell said in a soft voice. "Now, off you go, out of here."

When we went through the adjacent room, in which we had first met Riverblood, my gaze fell on the chalkboard. *Ruo Tultell* still stood written there in spidery letters. A strange feeling crept over me. I felt as though there was still a loose end that needed to be tied up.

Then the scales fell from my eyes.

"Oh, no way!" I said.

"What? What is it?" asked Marvin.

"Think about it: why was Riverblood so eager to sink the Star Runner with Ruo on board?" I asked.

"He wanted to sink the Star Runner because he never got the chance before. She was Lotterlulu's ship and he hated Lotterlulu. When we rediscovered the Star Runner, that was his opportunity. He restored it just so he could blow it up. Simple," said Lilli.

"But he was super excited when he thought he could sink the Star Runner with Ruo on it. As though that was something special. As though it made sense."

"Yes, you're right. Project Grand Slam," murmured Marvin. "Ruo was supposed to be on board. Shila said so."

"And it seemed as though Riverblood and Ruo knew each other. The way they talked..." I said.

"Maybe Ruo was someone who Riverblood blackmailed, too," said Marvin, and shrugged.

"Okay, but there's more. Let's assume that Riverblood had Ruo imprisoned but always intended to make it easy for him to escape. How could he be sure that Ruo would escape with the Star Runner? I mean, Ruo is an expert in all things Lotterlulu, but using a pirate ship as an escape vehicle?" I said. "That seems totally unlikely."

Lilli and Marvin furrowed their brows.

"Now check this out," I said, and pointed at the chalkboard. "Rearrange the letters!"

My two friends studied the writing, visibly thinking hard.

"It can't be!" Marvin yelled suddenly, clapping his hand to his forehead.

Lilli and Marvin both blurted out in unison: "Ruo is actually..."

# A New Beginning

Lotterlulu steered the Star Runner further and further out to sea. He had no intention of anchoring on the island. The children certainly wouldn't take much longer to put two and two together. And if he was lucky, they would convince Commissioner Hallewell to let him sail away for now. They seemed to know each other well, after all.

The sea was calm, the wind was ideal. Lotterlulu was wearing his old clothes, which he had discovered in the captain's cabin. Just like his ship, they had been perfectly restored. He was his old, young self once again.

Lotterlulu grasped the chain around his neck and looked at the shimmering green liquid in the pendant. Since Maria had been poisoned, he had waited many lifetimes for this moment. The Elixir of Youth.

Maria still lived. For all these years, Lotterlulu had used the Elixir of Eternity to keep himself and his love alive. Hidden on one of the thousands of Caribbean islands, asleep and a shadow of her former self, cared for by a small but highly trusted group of close friends.

Mankind had long since developed the technology and medication that could have freed Maria from the deep sleep induced by Riverblood's poison. But she would have awakened as an old woman, with black eyes and a black mouth.

No, Lotterlulu couldn't have wakened her. The shock would have been too great. But now he held a new hope in the palm of his hand.

It was only thanks to one of James Eckles' ingenious inventions that Lotterlulu had managed to steal two vials of the Elixir of Youth from Riverblood's stock aboard the Volante. The small remote-controlled metal spider could walk on walls and ceilings, swim, dive, and shoot sticky threads to hang down and swing itself from one place to the next. It could even grab small objects (like a vial full of elixir) and carry them safely away.

James Eckles believed he had given the spider to Ruo Tultell, the famous Lotterlulu researcher, so he could use it to explore the wreck of the Belle.

But Lotterlulu had used the spider for another purpose and stolen two vials of the Elixir of Youth. A little over a day ago, he had drunk his. The effect had been almost magical.

The pain in his old joints and bones disappeared. Suddenly, he no longer needed a cane to walk. He felt fresh strength flow into his muscles. Even the sight in his left eye, which he had lost to a sword cut when still a young pirate, came back completely. At about this time, he had met the kids at the harbor, introducing himself as Ruo Tultell. He had been using the alias for many years. It consisted of the letters of his pirate name, Lotterlulu.

In the hours that followed, his wrinkles had visibly smoothed out and the blackness in his eyes and lips had given way to a natural youthful tint. Even his sparse gray hair had grown thick and black. When he was Riverblood's prisoner in one of the many cells in the old cave prisons, his hair sprouted from his scalp so quickly that he could watch it grow.

Fortunately, his guards were careless. He was able to trick them, free himself and even change into one of their uniforms. To prevent anyone from easily identifying him as Ruo, he shortened his hair and beard as best he could, using an old pirate saber he found lying around. Now he looked like one of the many other henchmen that were running around in Riverblood's headquarters. And like a young man.

But when he suddenly saw Lilli in the Guardians' headquarters, that became a problem. He couldn't allow her to know his true identity, at least not yet.

Fascinated, Lilli had gazed down at the busy scene beneath the metal walkway. She hadn't yet noticed Lotterlulu, who had been standing in the shadows a few dozen feet away. He had acted quickly. Diagonally above him, a pulley hung from the ceiling, its wheels and chains covered with an oily black mass. With one hand he supported himself on the railing, with the other he reached the apparatus. He took a generous amount of the nasty oil and spread it through his hair, on the stubble of his beard and on the rest of his face - especially where his former wrinkles would have been visible.

His plan had worked. Lilli and later Timmi and Marvin had not asked too many questions.

Now he was finally alone on the Star Runner. He felt reborn. He would give the elixir to Maria, and when she was young again, he would wake her from her poisoned sleep.

Then he would slowly and carefully explain to her what had happened. So much to tell, of her long sleep and of how humanity had changed in the meantime. And that they would now have all the time in the world to finally grow old together.

Without elixirs.

And without living in fear of the Guardians. With the documents discovered and the evidence that would undoubtedly be found aboard the Volante, the organization was finished once and for all.

Just like Riverblood.

Maria and Lotterlulu would finally be able to enjoy their life together.

# CHAPTER 32

Riverblood was put on trial. We followed the proceedings with a lot of curiosity, hoping to learn more about the Guardians' schemes. It was like we had thought: The organization had branches all over the world, having built up a powerful network through bribery and blackmail. Thanks to Lotterlulu's documents, the ones we had discovered, and lots of painstaking investigative work, it was possible to trace the increase and migration of the organization's money over the past centuries. As a consequence, the organization could finally be completely dismantled. Riverblood received a long prison sentence.

But one thing puzzled us: Nothing about Riverblood's age, the elixirs, or Lotterlulu was mentioned publicly. When we asked Commissioner Hallewell if any other completed elixirs had been found on the Volante or if there were any records about how to make them, she only shook her head. "I'm sorry, but I don't know anything about it," she said, and her expression showed us that she didn't want to know, either. Someone very, very high up had probably decided to sweep the whole topic under the rug. Somehow that bothered me a lot. But I was glad for Lotterlulu, because it meant that no one would come looking for him and his Maria. Of course, I didn't know for sure that Maria was still alive, but I was pretty confident that the elixir in the pendant was meant for her.

Commissioner Hallewell was given a medal for her successful detective work. She looked really happy. She was soon off hunting for other serious criminals – but not before she took her first real vacation in a very long time.

A few weeks after Riverblood's trial ended, Lilli got a postcard. All that was written on it was "Thanks for everything!" next to a scribbled heart. According to the postmark, it came from Malta, and it had an unusual picture: a motorcycle next to the entrance to an office building. To judge by the sign over the door, it was the headquarters of an environmental organization that specialized in protecting the world's oceans. We were sure that this was Shila's way of saying farewell to us. Since the day of Riverblood's arrest, she had disappeared. Apparently, she had found new purpose in the meantime.

Sir London was entrusted with searching the remains of the pirate cave for ancient treasures that might have been spared during the volcanic eruption. In the harbor basin and the higher levels of the cave, he finally got lucky. He was able to reconstruct the turbulent history of the cave and create a museum dedicated to piracy on the island: the Lotterlulu Museum.

With the defeat of the Guardians, James Eckles no longer had to live under police protection. Since our last adventure, he had been in a witness protection program and had completely disappeared from the public eye. Now he finally returned to his penthouse in one of the most famous buildings in our city, called *The Sphere*, and dedicated himself to what he did best: inventing things!

### CHAPTER 33

# A Cup of Cocoa

It was a sunny morning as I knocked on the door of Lilli's grandpa's house. His white cat with orange stripes on her tail pranced around my legs. She probably wanted to come in, too.

"Hey there," I said. "You have at least one other way into the house, don't you?"

When no one opened the door, I took a step back and eyed the building. Lilli and Marvin were supposed to meet me here at ten in the morning. Where were they?

I knocked again, but there was no answer.

Puzzled, I trudged through the tall grass to the back of the house.

"Hello?" I called out loudly. In front of me was the wooden hatch that led to the house's coal cellar. This was where it had all started – our first Lotterlulu adventure, chasing the legend of the Star Runner. Since then, of course, it had been repaired.

Suddenly a small bird sat down on the hatch and watched me questioningly. It looked strange.

Hadn't I seen a bird like that somewhere before?

It fluttered up and hovered level with my face for a moment. Then it suddenly shot past me and flew deeper into the garden, away from the house and higher toward the crown of the mighty tree that stood at its center.

I squinted into the sun as I followed its flight.

And then I saw it: A large tree house, built high up on thick branches. Lilli and Marvin were sitting there, grinning down at me.

"Hey Timmi," Marvin called out. "Check this out."

To my amazement, the bird landed directly in Marvin's left hand. In his other, he held a remote control. "Isn't that crazy?"

Now I realized where I had seen the bird before: in the hall of James Eckles's flying machines! Back then, Lilli had held it in her hand and said that one day, she too would like to design something so wonderful.

"Come up!" she called, dangling a rope ladder.

"What is this place?" I asked when I had climbed up.

"Isn't it fantastic?" Lilli said excitedly. "Come in, it gets even better."

I was totally astonished. It looked like an office for detectives and adventurers. There was a table with chairs, a chalkboard, a sofa, a shelf full of books about famous mysteries, a radio, some lamps, blankets and everything else you need in a detective-adventurer's tree house.

"Wow, how cool!" I said.

"Awesome, right?" said Lilli.

"It's ours now, for all of us," Marvin said.

"Where did that all come from?" I asked.

"A present from James Eckles. As a thank you for helping to defeat the Guardians," Marvin said.

"Now he can finally do what he wants again, instead of hiding," said Lilli.

"And did he say what he has planned?" I asked.

"He said he either wants to go to Mars or to the future, but I think he was joking," Lilli said. "Anyway, he sounded happy."

"And he gave us the robotic bird that Lilli liked so much," said Marvin.

"And you of all people are controlling it?" I asked.

"Very funny. I'm the most experienced pilot here," said Marvin.

"Sure you are," I said with a grin. "You just destroy everything that you fly."

"Hello?" said a voice from below us. It was Lilli's grandpa. He was holding a small basket with cups and a thermos in it. "Would you like some cocoa?"

"Thanks, grandpa," Lilli said, beaming down at him.

"You're not up to more mischief already, are you? I hope you've had enough of adventures," he said.

"We can't help it, grandpa. Adventures just seem to find us," Lilli called down.

"Hmm, then hide from them for a little while," said Grandpa.

"We are. No adventure can find us here in the tree house," laughed Lilli.

I smiled happily, but deep down I hoped it wouldn't take too long. After all, what is life without adventure?

THE END

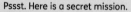

# FACTS FOR EXPLORERS:
## LEARN FASCINATING REAL-LIFE FACTS ABOUT THE WORLD OF EXPLORERS

# TIPS FOR
## ADVENTURERS & DETECTIVES:
### SECRET SKILLS AND FASCINATING EXPERIMENTS

# YOUNG EXPLORERS' SUCCESS BADGE!

## PLACE IT IN THE FRONT OF THE BOOK AND SHOW THAT YOU HAVE SOLVED ALL MYSTERIES.

# HINTS

Here you will find a hint for each chapter. The hints are written in mirror writing and are listed in reverse chapter order so that you don't accidentally read a hint for a later chapter.

### Chapter 30

**Fifth:** Riverbloom said he repurposed the casket. Find it!

**Fourth:** What was visible when Lilli met Kuno on the meadow walkway in the Guardians' headquarters?

**Third:** According to Shila, Riverbloom even gave his plan a name. Do you remember it?

**Second:** One of these details is something Riverbloom couldn't have known if he didn't know this employee.

**First:** Riverbloom said he didn't take anything from Kuno. Is that true?

Who entered an access code around the kids once before? What numbers have special meaning for this person? They were explained in a flashback.

First, slide the red modul one box to the right, so that modul 10 can be slid down. Now you can move modul 20 to the left and modul 30 all the way to the top. What should you do next?

**Chapter 27**

Look closely at the Star Runner in chapter 24 and compare the two pictures.

**Chapter 26**

The riddle refers to the title of the painting. That means it must have something to do with searching.

**Chapter 25**

An object that Kuo told Lilli about is in the picture. Can you find it?

**Chapter 24**

Look closely at Shila's motorcycle. Timmi lost something while he was escaping from the Carzdians. Do you see it?

**Chapter 23**

The hiding places must have enough room for Kuo and Lilli to completely hide themselves. Look at the far left and far right.

**Chapter 23**
BONUS QUESTION

There are smaller objects that are no longer in the same position as before. Look at the far right for one, and in the center for the other two.

**Chapter 22**

What is different between the man and the people below him? It may seem familiar to you.

**Chapter 21**

There is something in the picture that isn't from the time of pirates and that you have already seen once before in a photo.

**Chapter 15**

Some of the keys look like numbers.
What happens when you connect them in sequence?

**Chapter 16**

Look very closely at the three candles.
Do you notice a difference?
According to the riddle clue, which path must then be the right one?

**Chapter 17**

Look at the symbols on the cloth.
They will show you which symbols in the casket have to be connected.
The resulting pattern resembles one of the symbols next to the Latin words.

**Chapter 18**

Remember that the electricity allegedly went out moments before? The solution has something to do with light.

**Chapter 19**

The symbols on the sides of the casket don't seem to be complete.
Maybe you can find the solution if you put the two pages together and look from page 87.
Shine a flashlight against page 90.

**Chapter 20**

Look for two things that didn't exist during the time of pirates (at the lower and upper left).
And one thing shouldn't be there if all the houses were uninhabited (below, at center).

Use a mirror to read!

**Chapter 14**

Which lever can you turn so the shape stays the same
when you tip your head to the side?

**Chapter 13 — BONUS QUESTION**

Lotterjuju had to hurry, and something got stuck.

**Chapter 13**

Parts of the contraption that can trigger an alarm can be
seen in both of the two pictures.
Can you find them?

**Chapter 12**

What is the man holding on to, and where have you seen
it before?

**Chapter 11**

Many of the tourists seem to be reading.
Is there something unusual about one of them?

**Chapter 10**

Look around the cabin.
Were the two of them really alone?

**Chapter 9**

Look very closely at the photographs.
Is there a connection between what can be seen in them
and Konny?

**Chapter 8**

What did Marvin just learn about the island and its
vegetations?
Think about which parts ships couldn't have taken, and
why.

### Chapter 7

There are three clues.

Look closely at the boats and their surroundings.

Why are the boats blue?

### Chapter 6

Did it relate to one of the islands?

about the supposed firefate?

In the previous chapters, what information did we learn

### Chapter 5

Did something change?

Look at the picture on page 17.

### Chapter 4

Do you remember what it was?

Timmi had a chore after lunch.

### Chapter 3

What does a real fisher always keep in sight?

### Chapter 2

down.

Start by looking at the cliff below the hut and go all the way

find a shape somewhere in the rocks that is connected to its

What do we know about the legend of the caves? Can you

### Chapter 1

the boats?

Look at the picture on page 6. Is something different on

# THANK YOU

Without the support of my family and friends, I could never have written this book. First and foremost, I would like to thank my wife Anja for always supporting me with deep understanding and patience. On more than one weekend, family activities with our daughter Emmelie (who, by the way, is getting cuter and cuter) fell a victim to my writing. Lots of hugs and kisses!

❖ ❖ ❖

I would also like to thank everyone who read this book in its various stages of development – namely (in alphabetical order):

Dr. Markus Bruckner
Dr. Nicolas David
Albrecht Denzer
Martina Denzer
Sascha Gemming
Anja Wagner
Marie Wagner

Without you, this third volume would have been full of logical errors and contradictions. You saved me from writing about a ship that can sail against the wind without a motor, an invisible eternally burning candle, and even worms in a dark hedge and a broken puzzle box.

❖ ❖ ❖

Thank you, Javi, for your outstanding work, once again achieved in the face of looming deadlines. I think you are one of the most talented illustrators I have ever known, as you have proven once again in this new book.

❖ ❖ ❖

And many thanks to you, Elani, for your terrific translation. In contrast to previous Timmi adventures, this volume was first written entirely in German, and you succeeded in bringing this story brilliantly to life in English.

❖ ❖ ❖

Big, big thanks to Benedikt Gschaider and Grace Glowiak! Without your help, this text wouldn't have been nearly so refined and polished. You didn't just correct countless typos and grammar errors, but contributed many improvements to the writing and contents, too. Many thanks for your wonderful support!

❖ ❖ ❖

And last but not least, as always, special thanks go to my mom for being the best mom in the world and to my dad for telling me to do what makes me happy.

# FUN FACTS

This book contains a puzzle that is unrelated to the story and involves all thirty-one main illustrations. A hint to it can be found on the cover. Go to www.timmitobbson.com if you think you have the solution!

❖ ❖ ❖

Lotterlulu's love Anna Maria Is named after my wife's maternal grandmother, the president of the island Ingvar is named after my father, the archaeologist *Amilia* is named after my daughter's middle name, and the research vessel *Nostromo* is named after the space freighter from the movie *Alien.*

❖ ❖ ❖

The diving scenes of the drones and the archaeologists are also inspired by a scene from *Aliens*, in which *Ripley* can only watch the experiences of a team of explorers by video.

❖ ❖ ❖

The names *Monkey Island* and *Zak McKracken* in the Chapter 6 illustration refer to legendary video games from the late 1980s and early 1990s. This type of game is called a "point and click adventure." I loved them.

❖ ❖ ❖

If you'd like to learn much more about the inspiration behind Secrets of the Last Pirate, get the Fan-Package at https://www. timmitobbson.com. It's free!

# ABOUT THE AUTHOR

Jens I. Wagner lives with his beloved wife, his daughter Emmelie Amilia, and two big, orange cats right at the edge of a forest near Frankfurt, Germany.

He earned a master's degree at Oxford University where he loved being part of the Christ Church College community.

Jens is a fan of all kinds of fiction ranging from *Indiana Jones* to *James Bond*.